To An

The Eighth Continent
and other stories

by

Alba Ambert

*who lives with
me in the eighth
continent.
    Alba Ambert
    October 20, 1998
    New Haven*

Arte Público Press
Houston, Texas
1997

This volume is made possible through grants from the National Endowment for the Arts (a federal agency), Andrew W. Mellon Foundation, the Lila Wallace-Reader's Digest Fund and the City of Houston through The Cultural Arts Council of Houston, Harris County.

Recovering the past, creating the future

Arte Público Press
University of Houston
Houston, Texas 77204-2090

Cover illustration, Retrato familiar (a la Kahlo)
lápiz, 22"x30" 1991, by María Antonia Ordoñez
Cover design by James F. Brisson

Ambert, Alba N.,
    The eighth continent and other stories / Alba Ambert.
      p.   cm.
    ISBN 1-55885-217-4 (pbk.)
    I. Title.
    PS3551.M23E38   1997
    813'.54—dc21   97-22169
                                                                                           CIP

The paper used in this publication meets the requirements of the American National Standard for Permanence of Paper for Printed Library Materials Z39.48-1984.∞

Copyright © 1997 by Alba Ambert
Printed in the United States of America

This is a work of fiction. Names, characters, places and incidents either are the product of the author's imagination or are used fictitiously. Any resemblance to actual events or persons, living or dead, is entirely coincidental.

For Nicholasa Mohr

The following stories have been previously published:

"Dusks" in *The Americas Review*, Volume 17, No. 2, 1989; "The Old Language" in *The Americas Review*, Volume 21, No. 1, 1993.

Also by the Author:

Novels
A Perfect Silence
Porque hay silencio

Poetry
The Mirror Is Always There
Habito tu nombre
The Fifth Sun
Gotas sobre el columpio

Non-Fiction
Every Greek Has a Story: An Oral History

Children's Books
Why the Wild Winds Blow
Thunder from the Earth

I am grateful to:

My friends in Greece, whose love, friendship and companionship have made an enormous difference in my life. Angela Kiossoglou-Adams, Despina Meïmaroglou and Jennifer Michaelides, with whom I've shared the joys and sorrows of life and who understand the comforting properties of *tzatziki* and *patates tiganites*. Georgia Koumandaris, for our long afternoon talks; Constantinos Petrinos, for the many hours of storytelling; Eleni Doriza, who generously gave of her time to my work; Olympia Karayiorga for being the special person that she is; Varvara Tsipoura and Yiannis Karatzas, who made my life and work in Greece easier.

In other parts of the world and beyond, many thanks to Margarita Buila, whose caring and warmth help me in more ways than she knows. To Gay Young, for her lasting support. To Catherine Davidson, for the poetry that brought us together. To Morelia Bueno, for all that we've shared. To Professor Israel Sheffler, for his Saturday morning call and all that it meant. To Clemente Soto Vélez, who so often advised me: *métele fuego*. To Sara Meléndez, for our many years of friendship. To Sandra Pereira, for her love and concern. To Carlos Hernández Chávez, *mi hermano* and coconspirator in the work we know we must do. To Carmen Carrasquillo McCarthy, always present. To Nicholasa Mohr, sister survivor, who understands the pain and the joy. To Marina Catzaras, for meeting me on the path of words and walking it with me. To Isabel Oliveras, who gave me everything, and to Yanira Ambert, companion of a lifetime. To Walter McCann, for his love, understanding and optimism.

My deep appreciation to Richmond, The American International University in London, for offering the institutional support I need to pursue my writing.

Many thanks to Nicolás Kanellos, for believing in my work, and to the wonderful people at Arte Público Press, for their enthusiasm and hard work.

Finally, I'd like to thank my readers for their letters, words of encouragement, and support.

Mil gracias.

*Casi no puedo con el mundo
que azota entero mi conciencia.*

Julia de Burgos

Contents

The Eighth Continent 9
Dusks 27
Chupacabras, The Goat Sucker 37
The Wound 59
Letters to Mrs. Woods 85
The Old Language 91
The Curse 119
Rage is a Fallen Angel 137
"You Ain't Black You Ain't White
    You Ain't Shit" 159

The Eighth Continent

When Amanda began taking antidepressants, she stopped dreaming. Every morning at ten minutes to six, her eyes popped open, a sharp yellow or orange or red slicing through her clotted eyes. In the depths of sleep, she navigated the many folds of terror. The terror of knowledge without images. In her sleep, she knew a fear that she could never name when awake because there was no language for the absolute darkness of her fear. The darkness was so great, she sat up, wide awake in the middle of the night, heart hammering. Not knowing what frightened her, she would fall into a restless slumber again until dawn, when that familiar flash of yellow or red or orange blinded her. That was all sleep brought to her now. Darkness, terror and colors.

Amanda trembled under the blankets when the creak of the hallway stairs splintered through her wafer-thin walls. The tenement was settling into the daily cacophony of tired men and women lumbering down the stairs to the morning shift or kids scrambling to get to school on time. Her thoughts turned to Manolo until daylight drifted into her room. Late, as all the impunctual days of winter. She pushed the blankets away and stood on the cold linoleum. Shivering, she dressed quickly. In the kitchenette, she warmed her hands over the flame of the gas burner while on another hob she boiled water for coffee. She was startled when one of her neighbors clanged on the radiator to wake up the super. She blew into her cold hands and rubbed them briskly against each other.

There was no window in the small room that contained a kitchenette and an area for sitting and eating. She took her coffee to the only other room in the apartment and sat on her wicker rocker, next to a pile of books stacked on the floor. A table overflowing with papers leaned against her bed. It soothed her to look out the window, like a domestic cat, even though she had lost the ability to perceive distances in the neighborhood crowded with buildings. Through the windowpane speckled with old coats of paint, fingerprints and layers of dust, she could see a fire escape and under it an alley full of garbage and shards of glass. A rare morning breeze slithered between brick walls and swirled through empty beer cans, crumbled potato chip wrappers and dirty Styrofoam cups. When it was windy, the swish and jangle of debris clattering aimlessly barged tyrannically into her apartment day and night until it became as imperceptible as falling rain.

Amanda drained her cup of coffee and picked up a bottle of Algerian wine she kept by the bed. She licked her lips in anticipation as she filled the cup. She sipped slowly at first and then thrust her head back. The warmth rolled through her chest and settled pleasantly in her stomach. When she emptied the bottle, a fiery sensation flushed through her. It was pleasant, though. The lightheadedness, the swaying, the slight prickle of the skin. Her eyelids drooped heavily and her mouth slacked open. She stumbled into bed before passing out.

Amanda woke up at four when darkness was rapidly settling into the evening. She sat at the window again in her ritual contemplation of rubbish. The building across the alley was a massive six-story brick, peeling at the sides and edges, scrawled with red and black graffiti. Her favorite was the lament, *No sé quererte menos, no puedo quererte más.* I don't know how to love you less, I cannot love you more.

There was still slush on the ground when Manolo and Amanda arrived in Hartford, Connecticut, in late April, several years before. They had known each other since their university days in Puerto Rico. They fought bitterly the first year they were together because Manolo was born to a privileged San Juan family and Amanda accused him of never understanding the plight of the poor. She knew what it was like to go to bed hungry. To see her mother die in unbelievable pain because she could not afford a doctor. To have to beg university bureaucrats every year to increase her meager scholarship.

Though he was in no way responsible for the injustices of the world, deep inside, she made Manolo feel bad. She never thought she could fall in love with the enemy, someone who represented everything she loathed. She resented his privilege and took every opportunity available to point out how lucky he was compared to the wretched poor. And Manolo felt guilty. Provoking a man's guilt is an unforgivable sin. Men rarely forgive their mothers for it. Nor their partners.

There were times during that first year when they both wondered whether the differences in their backgrounds were too vast to breach. Once, during a particularly heated argument, Manolo shook his head sadly and said to her, "Maybe love isn't enough."

Amanda would never forget it. Manolo had become weary of her anger, her constant barrage against the injustices of the world. When she read about yet another injustice in the daily paper, she would sneak a suspect glance at him, as though he were responsible for the tortures, the secret human experimentation, the vices of humanity. She seemed to love and mistrust him at the same time. It was hard for her to trust. She had always been a silent woman, keeping her secrets to herself. Had been for years because she needed to live in her own mind. Only there could she avoid betrayal. Her mind was the only part of her that could not be penetrated against her will, the only part of her that felt protected.

Her mistrust wore on Manolo. He felt that he always had to prove himself to her, to prove his love, and with every test he passed, she managed to come up with a more difficult one.

Eventually her skepticism about his commitment subsided. They sealed a final pact of mutual trust when the independence movement asked them to settle in Hartford to continue working for the cause in the belly of the monster, as they called the United States. Manolo did not hesitate and neither did Amanda. Their lives were no longer their own. They worked day and night without respite in communities where life was harsh. Then Manolo was imprisoned and their lives spilled into the glare of public scrutiny. Nothing was private or sacred any longer. Strangers took their inner lives and poisoned them with their avid fingers, their crusty tongues. They contaminated all her belongings with their hands and poisoned her words with their breath.

"You left the door unlocked again. I can't believe this." Patricia bounded into the bedroom, her tall figure wrapped in a black coat. "I dropped in this morning before going to work and you were drunk again, Amanda. I couldn't wake you up. For Chrissake, drinking in the morning, it's a bit much."

Amanda sighed. "Hi, friend. What's new?"

"Don't get cryptic with me, young lady. Listen, Andrés is furious with you. You haven't submitted anything for publication in ages."

"It'll be ages before I do."

Patricia scanned the papers strewn on the table and spilling onto the floor. "Is there anything in here that's printable?"

"Only trash. I couldn't write a decent article if my life depended on it."

"But why?"

Amanda shrugged. "Inspiration has abandoned me. The muses no longer speak. I'm dried up."

"Don't give me that crap. You're not writing because you're drunk all the time. You have no willpower, that's all. And you have so much talent, Amanda. Don't you realize that you're letting a lot of people down?"

"Ha, that's hilarious. Who am I letting down? Tell me. I can't get anything published. Only Andrés will print my stuff. The world will survive without another commentator of daily life."

Elena walked into the room sniffing the air like a dog. "Hey, what's up, *muchachas*? Do I detect a little sauce around here?"

"Oh, shut up, Elena," Patricia said impatiently. "And what is this anyway, Grand Central Station? I swear, Amanda, a rapist is gonna walk into this place one day. I don't know why you're not double-locked like the rest of us."

"Because, my dear friend, I'm indestructible."

"Shit, now she's giving me the immortal poet routine." Patricia rolled her eyes to the ceiling. "Anything in the fridge? Looks like you could use a little nutrition."

Briskly, Patricia went into the kitchen and, humming an old *bolero*, raided the refrigerator with the intention of concocting some broth or soup, depending on the ingredients she could gather.

Elena sat at the edge of the bed and scratched the crook of her arm.

"*Chica*, I'm really down today. I think it's a hormonal down this time, you know, the real thing." She spread her tiny frame on the bed and stretched out as far as she could go, arms tucked under her neck. Then she slackened like a broken doll.

"No luck?" Amanda asked.

"Nothing. And I really try hard. I'll do anything for a job, take whatever comes along. But it's hard out there, *chica*. Don't know how much longer I'll last with the unemployment benefits running out."

Elena got up and poked her head out the bedroom door to make sure Patricia was in the kitchen. "I've got something for you," she whispered.

She dug into her pocket. Just as she was ready to hand something to Amanda, the women heard Andrés' voice. Elena sank her hand back into her pocket.

"Is everyone decent in here?" yelled Andrés, a little late, since he was already at the foot of the bed. Patricia rushed from the kitchen and kissed Andrés' black unruly beard, but she missed his lips hidden under the thick mustache. She tilted her head toward the other two women and raised an eyebrow. Andrés shrugged, dragged a chromium and oil-cloth chair from the dinette table and sat next to Amanda by the window. He had brought a six-pack with him. He tossed a beer to each of the women and drank deeply from his own.

"So, what's new, Amanda?"

"I don't know, but I woke up this morning with the strange sensation that the moon was dead," she said.

"Did you write it down?"

"No, I can remember it vividly enough."

"That's a great start, keep it up, *negrita*."

"What is this, creative writing workshop time?"

"Man, you haven't given me anything in months. People are asking about you. They think I won't publish your stuff. I'm getting a real bum rap on this one."

"Andrés, I can't write anymore. That's it. So don't bug me."

"Your problem. Heard anything from Manolo?"

"No correspondence allowed, remember?"

"Yeah, I remember. But, hey, maybe he can smuggle a letter out." Andrés flipped open another beer and drank deeply.

Amanda and Elena glanced at each other, then turned quickly to look out the window. A tiny shred of pewter sky could be seen from the window. It was cloudy with dust.

"Why all the long faces? Someone die?" Patricia poked her head in and laughed. "Soup's ready, anyone want some?"

"Did you put any meat in it?" Amanda asked.

"Where was I supposed to get meat? All you had in the fridge were some dried-out carrots and shriveled onions. Amazing how far a few bouillon cubes can go."

"I'll have some then."

"Yeah, me too." Andrés got up and dragged the chair back to the table.

When Patricia finished ladling the steaming soup into the bowls set around the table, Elena jumped up. "Got some bread upstairs, a little stale, but can't have soup without bread. Be right back."

Elena returned with the bread. She had replaced her jacket with a long, baggy shirt.

"Didn't know we had to change for dinner, like the British." Andrés eyed her as she sat down.

"Cat got hairs all over me. You know how it is with black."

"Get yourself a black cat," Andrés said.

"Oh, great, what's next, color-coordinated pets?" Amanda laughed. "Only you could think of it."

"Yeah, I'm busy thinking about a lot of things," Andrés said sourly.

"Like what?"

"You know, this whole business with Manolo. There's too much shit going down in all of this. It really stinks." Andrés dunked a slice of bread in the hot broth and slurped.

"Don't bring it up now." Patricia cast a nervous glance at Amanda.

"It's all right, Patricia. I've had a chance to think about little else but Manolo's predicament. Eight years in a federal penitentiary is a long time. With no correspondence, no visitors, in solitary confinement. Just imagining how he must feel makes me sick."

Patricia cut in quickly. "By the way, how's El Arcipreste doing? Haven't seen him in ages."

"He doesn't like to be called El Arcipreste. His name's something like Delta," Elena said.

"Not Delta, *boba*. His name's De Hita, Ramón De Hita," Andrés said. "We call him El Arcipreste to remind him of his lineage. But he thinks we're just making fun of him. Get a load of this: When I tried to explain that El Arcipreste De Hita was a great Spanish writer, he pulled out birth and baptism certificates from his wallet to prove to me that he was who he said he was. Thinks everyone's from the *migra* or something. Says he's from Bayamón, by the way. Ramón de Bayamón." Andrés leaned back and laughed. "Hey, Amanda, didn't know I was a poet did you? And my poems rhyme."

"Unfortunately, that's all they do," Amanda said. "Let's ask Ramón over for some soup. Is there enough?"

"Are you kidding?" Andrés said. "You know Patricia, she always cooks for a regiment."

"Not this time. There wasn't a lot in the fridge. We don't have much food upstairs either." She tossed a sidelong glance at Andrés.

"Don't look at me, I don't get paid till next Friday and we've got a lot of bills with the newspaper."

"When's that newspaper going to make some money?" Patricia asked.

"Not until we increase subscriptions and advertising. Maybe I can get a grant somewhere."

"I'll check it out in the library, see what's available," Patricia volunteered.

"Always count on a librarian to look everything up." Andrés patted Patricia on the head, and she jerked away from him.

"You know I hate it when you pat me like a dog," she said.

"I'm not patting you like a dog, like a little girl, *linda*."

"Well, I don't like it."

"Okay, okay, *mujer*," Andrés splayed his fingers. "Jesus, I'm surrounded by the *sensitivas*."

"Should I get El Arcipreste, I mean, Ramón, then?" Elena said. "He's probably outside melting someone's ears off. Can that guy talk!"

A few minutes later, Elena came in with Ramón in tow. Patricia served him some broth and then sat at a futon next to the dinette table.

"Hey, *amigo*, long time no see. How you doing?" Andrés got up, shook Ramón's hand and slapped him on a shoulder. "Sit down and have some soup with us."

"Oh, *gracias*." Ramón stood uncomfortably shaking his head from side to side. "But I didn't bring anything."

"Just sit down," Amanda said. "You've brought us your company, that's enough."

Amanda turned to Patricia. "What're you doing over there? Just bring another chair to the table."

"No, that's all right, I'm not really hungry right now."

"Must've stuffed yourself in the kitchen," Andrés mumbled.

Patricia lowered her chin to her chest as she always did when she was angry. "What're you talking about?"

"I know you're a secret eater. Going through the fridge at three in the morning. It's no wonder we don't have anything left to eat."

"There was nothing here either."

"Well, you must have binged on chocolate or something on your way home from work. I tell you, you're not gaining all that weight from dieting."

"Thanks a lot." Patricia crossed her arms over her chest and tapped her feet. Her face was set in a scowl.

Abruptly, Ramón started digging in his pockets and pulled out some folded papers from in his wallet.

"Look, these are my birth and baptism certificates. You see, it says here that I was born in Bayamón, Puerto Rico." He stood up and presented the papers to each person at the table.

"We know who you are," Amanda said. "We're not the enemy, you know."

"I know, I know, but some people get confused." Ramón was mollified and dropped into the chair. "They think we're all illegals. Andrés here thought I was some kind of Spaniard."

"All your papers are in order, Ramón. I'm sure you'll be okay." Andrés pushed another beer in his direction. "Sorry I confused you with a Spanish writer, my man."

Elena started giggling uncontrollably.

"What's so funny?" Ramón said with agitation.

"Oh, don't make me laugh," Elena said, gasping. "I get asthma when I laugh."

"Well, I don't know what's so funny. I'm no Spanish nothing. I want to make that clear to everyone. I'm not going to sit here and listen to these epitaphs."

"You mean epithets?" Patricia asked.

"Names, names, that's what I mean."

"Hey, calm down. No one's calling you anything." Amanda got up and followed a wheezing Elena to the bathroom.

"At the factory they listen to everything we say. Spies everywhere." Ramón was now pacing the tiny room from one corner to another.

"Never mind that now." Andrés got up to get some more of the beer he had stashed earlier in the refrigerator. "How's Elena?" he asked Amanda when she returned.

"Took a whiff from my inhaler. She's okay." Amanda uncorked another bottle of her Algerian wine. "This is the best remedy against this cold place. Come on, Ramón, sit down and try some of this wine."

"Okay, okay," Ramón said stiffly. "I just get upset about some things."

"What'll we toast to?" Patricia tried to steer the conversation away from Ramón.

"To profanity," Andrés said promptly, lifting his beer can.

"I toast to anything that's prolonged," Patricia said, suddenly cheered. She raised her eyebrows at Andrés and laughed.

Amanda saluted Patricia with her wineglass. "And to prophesies and proverbs and proletarians and prose and poetry."

Elena came to the table again, rubbing her chest. "Oh, no, don't get her started," she laughed and coughed.

"A toast to promiscuity," Andrés said and gave Ramón two slaps on the back. "Hey, Ramón, how about you? What inspires you, man?"

Ramón looked into the bottom of his glass. "I don't know any fancy words, " he said. "All I know is fear."

Amanda's smile faded. "Well," she said, "I toast to the eighth continent, then. The place all of us here have come to inhabit."

"What do you mean by that?" Elena asked.

"The eighth continent is for people who don't belong where they are nor where they came from. Like us. We don't belong here and we don't belong there."

"Speak for yourself," Andrés responded heatedly. "We're going back to Puerto Rico as soon as we can. Right, Patricia?"

Patricia nodded vigorously.

"Think you'll be the same person who left?" Amanda asked.

"So what if I'm not."

"That's what I mean. There's no way we can return from the eighth continent. Even if we wanted to. We think we can go back to what we left, but what we left is no longer there. And we're not the same people we were when we arrived. So we stay here, where we don't belong anyhow."

"You talking about illegals?" Ramón asked apprehensively.

Amanda warmed to her subject. "Illegals, all immigrants everywhere in the world, marginal people."

"How about crazies?" Elena asked.

"Oh, yeah. And eccentrics, too," Amanda said. "Anyone who for one reason or another doesn't belong, inhabits the eighth continent. A place with a boundary that can't be recrossed. There's no return possible from the eighth continent. There's no way out," she added.

"Man, Amanda, you're really getting me down." Andrés shook his head and drained his beer can.

"Yeah," Elena said. "That's real depressing."

"Okay, okay," Amanda said, raising her hands. "I give up. If you don't want to face the truth, let's change the subject."

Andrés turned to Ramón. "Hey, maybe you can help us with our campaign."

"What do you mean?" Ramón asked suspiciously.

"You must have heard. The campaign to free Manolo. We've got letters with hundreds of signatures going everywhere, Congress, the UN Decolonization Committee, you name it."

Amanda pushed her soup bowl away, slowly, deliberately. Her mouth set firmly in a fine line.

"Andrés, as long as the mainstream media pay no attention to our situation, no one's going to care. No matter how many signatures you get or how many articles you write. Who reads *El Alba* anyway? A handful of Puerto Ricans and the FBI."

"I read it," Elena chimed in.

"My point exactly. An unemployed Puerto Rican woman living a marginal existence, you're a good prototype of the readership I'm talking about. Who cares about what you read, what you think, what you feel? Who cares about any of us? We're the invisible people."

Elena looked at Amanda warily, not certain whether she should take offense. She scratched the crook of an arm and stared at the checkered tablecloth.

"Listen, Amanda," Andrés glowered. "I'm real tired of your attitude. We're working damn hard to effect some changes around here, and what do we get from you? Nothing. You're drunk all the time, don't contribute a thing to the cause. What the hell's the matter with you?"

"No, you listen, Andrés," Amanda pointed a finger at him. "I was locked up for a long time. You don't know what that's like."

"Calm down, Amanda, he didn't mean anything," Patricia cut in uneasily.

Amanda ignored her. "And where were you when they locked us all up, anyhow?" Amanda asked Andrés. "How come you came out of that interrogation room so quickly and the rest of us wound up in jail?"

"Ah, excuse me," Ramón cried anxiously. "You were in jail? Interrogated?"

"Don't you know what happened here last year?" Elena turned to him.

"Are you people drug pushers or something?" Ramón's eyes were wide with fear.

Elena giggled, this time nervously. "Not drugs. Politics."

"Oh, my god, that's worse!" Ramón rushed to the door. "I shouldn't be talking to you people. I hope no one saw me come in. Listen, I'm sorry, but I gotta go."

Patricia rushed from the table and grabbed Ramón by the wrist. She dragged him back. "You're not going anywhere. Just sit down and relax, will you?" she ordered. "God, you're capable of turning us in to the police."

"You got a gun?" he looked up at Patricia, eyes round as dinner plates.

"Just calm down, okay? We haven't done anything wrong."

"Okay, okay." Ramón swallowed hard.

Andrés paced the floor furiously. "I don't believe this. Are you implying, Amanda, that I was somehow responsible for your being detained for further interrogation?"

"Detention is a euphemism for where they put us and what they put us through, Andrés. And you know it. At least Manolo had the semblance of a trial. The rest of us were, as they say, 'under suspicion,' but they locked us up just the same."

Amanda trembled as she poured more wine. She took a quick swig from her glass and looked into it. Her shoulders hunched forward, her face set into a hard mask. When she spoke, her voice was hard-edged and bitter.

"Murderers have more rights than we have. They're certainly treated better. You have no idea what they did in there. Treated me like a slab of meat. There isn't a bodily orifice of mine that wasn't violated. You don't know anything, Andrés. You weren't there."

Andrés looked at Amanda angrily. He sat down to take another drink. "Shit, Amanda, you're blaming me now because I wasn't detained?" He turned to Patricia. "Can you beat that?"

"I'm not blaming you for anything. I'm just saying you have no idea what it was like for me and the other people detained, and you have no idea what it's like for Manolo, the scapegoat who's been sacrificed for all of us."

"Wait a minute. Please," Ramón interrupted with the palms of his hands held up in front of his chest. "What's this all about?" Then he leaped out of the chair again. "No, never mind, I don't want to know nothing. I just wanna go home."

"But it was in all the newspapers and on the news," Patricia said.

"I don't watch the news. I don't want to know nothing," Ramón yelled. "Just leave me alone, I don't want to get involved with you people."

As Ramón stormed out, Elena got up.

"I better go see what he's up to," and she followed him down the stairs.

Andrés shoved back his chair and it fell over. He said to Patricia, "We better go too." Then he turned to Amanda. "I hope you didn't mean what I think you meant, because if you did, you're questioning my loyalty and I won't have it."

"Andrés. I'm not saying it was you who spilled the beans. I'm just saying that you were the only one who wasn't detained."

"You drunken bitch! How dare you accuse me of anything?"

Amanda looked at him wearily. "Get out of my house," she said quietly.

Andrés slammed the door behind him. Patricia came up to Amanda and put a hand on her shoulder. "Don't do this, Amanda, please."

"Sorry, Patricia, you have to live with him, but I don't. If you don't trust what I'm saying, just look at the facts."

"Are you coming, or not, Patricia?" Andrés yelled from the hallway.

"I'll be right up."

"Whose side are you on anyway?" Andrés bellowed.

Patricia opened the door. "Andrés, please don't yell like that. All the neighbors can hear you. I'll be right up, I said."

"You better come with me this minute, or we're finished. Finished, you hear?"

"Don't put me in this situation, Andrés."

"You taking the side of that *puta* over me?"

Patricia turned to Amanda and said quickly. "I better go, Andrés is a little drunk and you know how irrational he gets."

"Don't make excuses for him," Amanda said. "Just go."

Amanda shut the door and made sure it was double locked. In the bathroom, she splashed cold water on her face until she was wide awake and alert. She pushed the mildewed plastic curtain aside and sat on the bathtub rim. There were cracks and yellow stains of humidity seeping through the stained walls. She stretched toward the tiled wall surrounding the bathtub. She nudged the edge of a tile with a nail file and carefully removed it. Amanda reached into a narrow pit gouged into the wall and with her thumb and forefinger pulled out a wad of toilet paper.

She sat on the toilet seat and reread Manolo's smuggled letter. He was beaten frequently and suffered sensory deprivation. He feared for his life. Someone had betrayed them. Only Elena, who was one of their couriers, could be trusted. They should both be careful. He loved her.

Amanda kissed the letter and tore it into tiny bits before flushing it down the toilet. Elena had brought Ramón to have dinner as a distraction and she had faked the asthma attack to get the message to her. She realized the paper showed over her narrow jacket pocket and changed to a baggy shirt. Andrés and Patricia had no idea Elena was a member of the most clandestine cell of the movement. Nor would they ever know, if Amanda could help it.

Amanda took her nightly Elavil with a gulp of wine and lay fully clothed on her bed. In thirty minutes flat, she would be asleep, tossing and turning with her night terrors. She had never anticipated living in the eighth continent, the place of perpetual banishment. She prepared for sleep from the frontier of an inevitable exile. She was caught drifting aimlessly in a continent of marginal people, all coming together in a babble of languages, a cacophony of traditions, but never quite merging with any sense of belonging. Always looking back, far back, to the impossible return.

Amanda drifted to sleep with nothing to wait for but the sharp yellow or red or orange that would startle her in the morning.

Dusks

She's buried in a potter's field somewhere. Her name was Isabel, like the queen. She wasn't regal though. She was a shantytown-dwelling seamstress who died of tuberculosis when I was two. Perhaps I witnessed her death and that is why I will forever wonder about silence. That was a long time ago, another life. I've lived so many lives since then, I sometimes feel trapped in a parade of windows. A friend says I have more lives than a cat. She may be right, though my lives seem more like dreams and nightmares. Today I sit here watching dusk collect silently in corners and know that this too will be a dream one day. Dusk always falls tied to events. If I say: Remember that dusk when David stumbled in with a broken nose? we all understand that dusk.

This is my mother's dusk for tonight; for some reason, I feel the painful presence of her absence. She loved me so. I know because her hugs were hard and gentle and I can still feel them soothe the edges of hurt and turn the tears away like scolded children. My father did not love her. Nor me. So we clung like earth snails to our own love, our carapaces shields against his quiet cruelty. His name is Benjamin. Bad man, bad man. He later confessed he thought I was a frog when born, and turned away, his back an accusation. In the hardscrabble barrio, swollen like a pigeon's chest, he strutted into other women's beds, while my mother waited. A rancid candle scrawled her shadow on the walls of the squalid shack. Her chest was red with blood, her cough blue with hurt. He did not see her buried. Strangers did it for him.

Someday I'd like to hold it up to his face. But someday is too long to gather tears. And besides, she's no longer here, so what does it matter? She no longer sees or knows or touches or feels. Yet there is so much love for her in me with no place to root, for it is only hers, like fingerprints. If she could only see her tall granddaughter who looks nothing like her, but then neither do I who bear the curse of my father's image carrying forth forever the face that detested her and me.

Her granddaughter is grown now, taking tentative steps in the world's marshes. We clung to each other too, like vines, and grew strong by sucking the hearty sweat of love. And then she was torn from me because her weight could only bring me down. It hurt deep in my womb where the deepest pain is felt. She hurt too, though her pain is young and sweetened by expectations. Life will be good to her, I know.

It has been good to me too, at last. I hobbled and stalked and roiled from shantytown to ghetto to village to city, thirsting for something better. My days were in my hands like froth and I spit stones into them and made them hard and smooth. And I met love after so many others squandered golden dusks amid a rattle of false runes. There was the bearded one of whom my mother would never approve, with his manly whimpers of disappointment. His mewl spattered like hot grease and I grew weary. There was the married man who collected nine of my years like calling cards in his attaché case. He was a handsome one, tall and dark like the moon and bold as an arrow. But waiting does not become me and the sentence stretched my frustration until it thinned and snapped and I lashed out and fled in a whirl of rejection.

Before them, in a life so distant I have trouble remembering its ocean-scattered dots of light, there was my daughter's father. His also was a quiet cruelty that closed a circle I dared not break until many lives later. He guzzled and sucked and grabbed and loomed above me like a genearch. He pocked my self-esteem with muck and I hung still as a spent rag, torn in ruminations. I broke the circle one day and then broke others. Destined to the life of my mother, I became an educated woman instead. To make her proud, to compensate somehow for the pain I caused her by arriving buttocks first, ripping her open like a seam. Yet she still loved me. I only understood that love when my own daughter ripped my darkness and cast her scream into my world. It takes that long to understand.

I will never understand my mother's death, though. When she died, silence and loneliness roared like an empty shell. And then the voices settled in me, piercing, intruding. Your mother's with God now, they said in their black dresses, and I knew they lied. The sun was sharp that day. It could have been any month in the endless summer of Puerto Rico. I ran into every nook and crawled under the dusty haze of her cot. Where could she be? How could she breathe or talk or eat if not with me? How could I see without her eyes? I had only known myself through her. How could I breathe or talk or eat if she was gone? Eyes stitched like wounds, I cried for her until they took me away in a black bundle.

Auntie Andrea took me in. She was my mother's aunt and very old. I sat in her lap in the afternoons when the sun was too hot to play outside and dust lay dry as dead bones and just as quiet. Sometimes a dog barked or a confused cock sprung a weary crow. I felt content in her ample lap. She licked her middle finger and turned the pages of her Bible as she mumbled the lines slowly. At times she lifted a page and with her thumbs divided it in two. Miraculous. How could she create new pages this way? I slept to her mumbles until heavy feet slapped against the bare wooden floor and I ran and squatted under the shack with the chickens until the pounding feet were heard on the creaky wooden steps and dust rose on the road. It was Auntie Andrea's son. I have since forgotten his name. Then she would call Blanca, Blanquita, and I knew there would be peace.

At night he staggered into the shack. When he did not see me, he did not remember me. But if he returned early or rose from his bed before I escaped, he would have his sport. Auntie Andrea was afraid of him too. She would wait until he left or slept to pull out a wooden crate she hid under her bed. In it she stored tiny tins of unguents, a eucalyptus alcohol she concocted herself, a framed Saint Jude and her Bible. Every night before we climbed into her bed, she mumbled to the picture and crossed herself many times. On a bad day, she would pry a tin open and anoint my bruises. The cigarette burns required more extensive treatment, so she combed the fields at dawn for black calabash leaves, and crushed, patted them on the injured skin amidst mumbled prayers and warnings.

The Arecibo village shone in the noon heat when a rare automobile stumbled on the narrow dirt road and lifted its gravel-filled voice. Barefoot children with bare buttocks gathered round the long dusty car. A big man sprang from the dust. Squatting under the shack with the chickens, I saw his heavy shoes approach. Many feet pounded above me, some with the sharp edge of shoes, others muted. Then I heard Auntie Andrea call. Blanca, Blanquita.

The man looked vaguely familiar. He slurped black coffee from the only glass cup in our possession. It was white with pink flowers. Auntie Andrea drank from a tin can. Her son sat on his cot and smoked. So this is the girl, she's getting big, the man said. What's the matter, don't you recognize your own father? Years later he told me this story many times with some degree of resentment. Why he would resent my lack of recognition, I will never understand, but for some reason he thinks I owe him my life. He said he'd take me for a ride in the long dusty car. Liar, liar. I loved cars, their speed, their deep rumblings, the hot wind blowing my hair back, the acrid smell of gasoline. I kissed Auntie Andrea quickly, not knowing I would never see her again.

I cried that night for her and cried for days and many nights afterwards. Where are we going? I asked my father, and he responded cryptically. I wondered what a new york was. Auntie Andrea would certainly know. She knew many things. She knew the mysteries of the full moon and the evil eye and she could interpret the neat marks in a book. She'd look up at the sky, eyes squinting, and say, A storm is brewing, and the thick air would roll away. The sky would darken, mumbling louder than Auntie, and the wild winds would climb our steps and hurl into the shack through wooden boards, jostling the kerosene lamps. And the rain would clatter on the zinc roof and spill through the rafters like an angry mob. Auntie Andrea would scurry about with the buckets and pans and rags she had prepared. Because she knew.

I cried and called for her that first night in New York and cried even more the next day when my father's mother said I would be living with her now and Auntie Andrea was far, far away. New York, hateful New York. It was a dark, dirty place, stuffed with tall houses with many windows and many doors. The doors were always locked. When I peeked out the window, there was no brilliant sun that made your eyes squint and your skin lay still and quiet, drinking its heat. No one smelled like sunshine in New York. It was dingy, the colors muted like a faded flag. What I hated most, though, was the old woman who claimed she was my mother now. She had my father's blue eyes and his curly hair and she never read or sat me in her lap. She spanked me when I cried and made me call her *Mami*. It was so hard because my real *Mami* was fresh in my memory. I could still smell her warm skin and feel the smoothness of her flesh. Her breasts were round and fluffy and I'd spend hours squeezing them while she sang in her rocker. The old woman had skin I did not want to touch. It was red and rough and her breasts hung limp over her abdomen like pierced balloons.

Day in day out like sewing needles. The fabric of the South Bronx spread, and tamped its texture into me forever. What a terrible thing forever is. I am trapped in the history, dark and drab and damp, of this gutted basement swollen with rats. We all scurried about, nostrils flaring. Day in day out.

P.S. 34 and P.S. 9. A Spanish-speaking Puerto Rican girl in the South Bronx, my education began in a class for the mentally retarded. Mysteriously, I was no longer retarded when I learned English. So plucked from my dim-eyed friends, I entered a class where I finally learned to read—in the language I knew least. The first-grade class read out of sheer fright, for the teacher, a dark-haired woman with scarlet nails, pulled at our collars and braids and dug her red nails into our arms. To consolidate her power, she boasted possession of two eyes behind her head, hidden under her hair, so even when facing the blackboard, she could see our every move. We cringed and read, trembled and wrote, threw-up and computed until summer gratefully saved us from the scarlet-nailed tyrant.

It was difficult to concentrate in school. We were always hungry. Then they gave us free breakfast and lunch and it was not so hard. I learned to read so well, I was sure to have equaled the magical Auntie Andrea. I also sank into the depths of books and listened to their hidden chants. There were no books at home, so I read tomato sauce labels, billboards, anything. I stood for hours in front of the newspaper stand and gulped the words until intoxicated. The attendant always knew I was there. He would shoo me away like a fly, and like a fly I'd zoom back for my honey. One day he asked me my name and I said Blanca. And he said, that's a pretty name, it means white doesn't it? I said, yes, how do you know? And he said, oh, I know many things. Which surprised me, because he was blind.

One day a cousin arrived from Puerto Rico and brought with her a book. She recognized my hunger and offered it to me like a sacrament. I avidly spread its pages before me, but I couldn't read, for it was in Spanish. Hungry, I pored over my first book. I searched through its pages and scrutinized the drawings. Then I went back to the first page, the first sentence, the first word, the title. Familiar letters, letters I knew, words that I knew too, but did not know I knew. Oh, the pain, the pain of those intractable symbols. I wanted to possess them, pierce them, drink them, devour them. My hunger for them did not wane. I held the book tightly, the words wiggled and swam and titillated. Then I split the words like ripe pomegranates and spilled the letters like seeds. I gently gathered the seeds into their shells one by one, again and again, over and over, until each word burst in my mind like a blossom. The world would never be the same after that.

It was a good thing I taught myself to read in Spanish because we returned to Puerto Rico one day and I could read and discuss *El Laberinto* with the best of them. A return to the womb, that's how it was. My mother's presence was stronger there where the sun almost always shines and flowers peek through stones. I had never seen a Puerto Rican teacher before, or a Puerto Rican physician, or a Puerto Rican attorney. When I gazed at their high intelligent brows, I thought, I can be one of them because they are like me and I am like them. I don't have to be Jewish or Irish or Chinese to be a doctor or a lawyer or a teacher or a pharmacist. What do you know? I was truly amazed.

The true struggle began because we were poor and it was tough to scratch the earth for words. So I took secretarial courses in high school because I knew I had to work to reap a sunrise. Anticipation of History of the World 101 quelled the boredom of Gregg Shorthand. Miguel de Cervantes, whom I met at university night courses, stoked my mind with stars as I typed legal briefs, eight hours a day, after delivering *The San Juan Star* at dawn.

I know she was there through it all. The sleepless nights, the migraines after exams, the birth of my child, my divorce, my diplomas. My pain, my want, my joy, my weary dusks. I felt her presence in averted disasters, the tug that woke me when I lay down to die. It was also dusk. A time when all is still and shreds of light sigh and burst into the deepest blue. The stillness is so great, so lonely, thoughts pound relentlessly, unstifled at last by daily tasks and routine conversations. On one such dusk the weight of all that lives and all that dies quietly crushed me. I willed to die under its screaming burden, and I lay in bed staring at the white ceiling. Then I closed my eyes, swept by oblivion. But a presence pulled me to the surface with a strong and gentle hand. I know she was there because it was not my time. Though the clock struck twelve on the darkened soil and beckoned with its hollow echo.

Now that I have learned to like the dusk, I need her still. She could share my placid life and we could bask together like kittens in the sun. She would approve of her granddaughter's timid attempts at independence, a possibility she never envisioned because she was a woman and she was poor. She would approve of the partner who chases my nightmares and the cries of terror that still besiege me. I wish she were here now to share with me my quiet triumphs. I'd give her flowers on her birthday. Anemones and hyacinths.

But I don't know where she lies. Her white bones bare, her tired heap alone.

Chupacabras, The Goat Sucker

(THE INCREDIBLE STORY OF THE INGENIOUS DOÑA FERMINA BELTRÁN, HER OBSESSION WITH NORTH AMERICAN TELEVISION TALK SHOWS AND THE UNEXPECTED FATE THAT RESULTED FROM HER PASSION FOR ORCHIDS.)

Fermina rocked steadily in her mahogany chair and stared at the TV set that one of her four daughters, Mariluz, had given her for Mother's Day after the one Fermina brought from New York, when she and her late husband Neftalí moved to Puerto Rico, conked out. The commercial break over, Geraldo's deep voice filled the living room. Fermina canted forward, feet firmly planted on her Spanish-tiled floor, rocking-chair gliders tipped to the ceiling. She turned her good ear toward the TV and distractedly petted one of her five cats: the sleek, slate-gray Cervantes, who napped placidly on her lap.

On today's show about sexual addiction, a young blond—quite ordinary looking, Fermina judged—described her multiple trysts with strangers in shopping mall parking lots, where she would pick up her more-than-willing partners. Every single day the blond needed a fix. She'd had sex with hundreds of anonymous men, she said. Oh, no, the young woman shrieked when Geraldo asked, my husband doesn't know. He will now, Fermina chortled. Greta, the part Persian, part who-knows-what, looked up at Fermina with eyes like slits from her favorite spot on the sofa, where she spent half her life, removed from the other cats, sleeping.

Earlier in the day, Oprah had interviewed transsexuals, both male and female. Fermina had a hard time keeping track of who had been what because the men who had operations to become women then fell in love with other women and the women who became men went on to fall in love with other men.

"¡*Virgen María Santísima!* They supposed to be gay?" Fermina asked the TV and shook her head not understanding this conundrum at all. "Maybe they really are what they were and that make them not-gay, huh? That what I think!" she informed Oprah in no uncertain terms. In her excitement, she rocked back, crunching poor Ewok's fat tail with the chair glider.

"*Ay,* I'm sorry, Eee-goo-ah."

Mariluz's son had named the cat and Fermina could hardly pronounce his name. Grunting, she picked up the twelve-pound cat, gave him a few rubs under the chin and poured some milk in a saucer. As soon as she sat down again, Cervantes had homed into her lap.

Fermina hated it when someone on a talk show was shouting at someone else, usually something juicy, and time ran out and the station started running the credits. Fermina couldn't catch what the blond nymphomaniac was shouting to a member of the audience. Frustrated, she zapped off the TV with her remote, until the next talk show was on later in the day. While Cervantes kneaded on her cushioned belly, Fermina shook her head thinking about the difficulties of intercourse in shopping mall parking lots. What do they do with all those arms and legs? She asked herself and thought of her late husband Neftalí, may he rest in peace. He never demanded too much from her in that department. All he wanted was some coochie, coochie once in a while. But when he had a little too much Palo Viejo while he watched Iris Chacón on TV, he'd always get frisky and it took him forever to finish. But she didn't mind, even when she knew it was Iris Chacón's formidable buttocks that were pinned to his mind.

Neftalí had been a good hard-working man who always provided for her and their daughters. His face was rugged, like a mountain surface, but he was a gentle soul. Just as he turned sixty, and after all the daughters had finished university, they bought the long-dreamed-for *finquita*, a little farm, and settled in Barrio Esperanza, Canóvanas. They were glad to be away from cold, dreary New York, even though two of their girls stayed behind. But Mariluz, the chemical engineer, and Graciela, the general practitioner, came to Puerto Rico with them once they finished their studies. Mariluz was now divorced with teenage twins—a boy and a girl—and worked at a pharmaceutical company in Carolina. Fermina was always lighting candles to a framed picture of Saint Anthony that she kept upside down on her dresser to guarantee a new husband for Mariluz. Graciela, thank her lucky stars, was okay. She married a surgeon and they both worked at the Fajardo Municipal Hospital and had private practices in the city. But after five years of marriage, they still hadn't given Fermina more grandchildren.

While Neftalí farmed, Fermina took care of the house and tended to her pride and joy: the lushest, most lavish, sumptuous, fragrant orchid garden Canóvanas had ever seen. Neftalí built a shed behind the kitchen, where Fermina repaired whenever she could to commune with her little darlings. In the shed she made sure they could bathe in the necessary light, yet be protected from the inclement tropical sun. Every morning before breakfast, Fermina inspected the clusters of richly hued petals. She loved the colors, their satiny sheen brighter than any jewel. Amethyst, fuchsia, lavender, crimson, indigo, golden yellow, dazzling white. She fingered the soft petals gently. If she closed her eyes, she could identify each plant by the texture of its leaves and petals. They were feathery or waxy or leathery or ruffled at the edges like elegant gowns. Delicate aromas rose with the humidity as she watered the spongy bark compost or moss where the orchids thrived. She loved the graceful symmetry of each flower, the way the lip nodded daintily toward the roots, like a nostalgic trumpet. Some resembled little ears, others fiddles or horns. They reminded her of tiny, defenseless animals, like all the cats she had picked up over the years.

The only troubles that marred Fermina's life in those days, and which continued to this very day, were Don Jacinto's goats. Don Jacinto, the irascible owner of the *finca* adjoining theirs, allowed his goats to wander into neighboring parcels of land, where they chomped up everything in their path. Sometimes Fermina would be watering her delicate lady slippers when the unmistakable stench of old goat would make her nose screw up in disgust.

"*¡Fo, qué peste!*" She'd run out pinching her nose with one hand and shooing the goats with the watering can in the other. "What a stink these *cabras* make, *por Dios!*"

She had tried everything to make Don Jacinto take responsibility for the goings-on of his *cabras*. She even reported him to the Humane Society. Surely, allowing goats to dine on orchids consisted of the most brutal cruelty. Why, some of the orchids could be poisonous. Couldn't they? Or at least cause serious intestinal problems. But no. They wouldn't take her complaints seriously. "Lady, we got people torturing horses around here. Starving and beating them to death. We know Don Jacinto and he takes good care of his goats." (Everyone knew everyone in the small town. Unfortunately.) "What do you want from us?"

Neftalí, who didn't want to cause any trouble—he was that kind of man—put up a fence between the two properties and sealed it with chicken wire. The goats always managed to jump over the fence, though. They could really leap, those sons of...of... old goat.

Other than the trouble with Don Jacinto's goats, Fermina had been happy in their retirement. She was finally living like a lady of leisure. In New York, Neftalí had been a repairman for the telephone company. He made good money and was frugal. They bought a small brick house in Queens and educated their daughters at state universities. Fermina cleaned houses in more affluent neighborhoods. With her earnings, Fermina bought fabrics to sew her own and her daughters' dresses and helped with other household expenses.

Neftalí would not waste a penny. He never had a beer with his fellow workers at quitting time nor did he ever buy an unexpected gift for Fermina. Graciela used to say that he was tighter than a scared mollusk. Whatever that was. But Fermina thought he was more like a clam. Small, but muscular, all he needed to be happy were his three meals a day, not counting snacks at ten and three.

The years took the edge off Neftalí's frugality. Or at least that's what Fermina thought after they sold everything they owned in New York and acquired their farm and she developed a passion for orchids. Neftalí bought a car, built her orchid shed and seemed more relaxed about money. He started saying that they could not take their money to the grave, so they might as well enjoy it. But then, when she least expected it, his overabundant frugal genes acted up again.

One fateful day, Neftalí, who had started to institute some stringent economic measures in the *finca*, decided to artificially inseminate one of his cows himself. When he shoved an arm sheathed in a long plastic glove into the cow's private parts—all the way to the elbow—the cow did not take kindly to this defilement and kicked Neftalí so hard, he was last seen alive soaring through the air, right arm sticking up and smeared with a reddish viscous substance Fermina could not identify at the time. Poor Neftalí, may his soul rest in peace, landed with a thud, head first, into a pile of cement blocks he had purchased to build a kitchen extension. The cow didn't even get pregnant. At least not due to Neftalí's efforts.

"Ay, Neftalí, *m'ijo,* if you could only see how fat the cow is now." Fermina looked up to the ceiling while Cervantes continued kneading—he was a championship kneader.

"Got her a young bull from a neighbor and he did the job real easy. It don't cost so much either. Been calving ever since. I wish you had not been so thrifty. It always got you in trouble. Remember that time, *mi corazón,* when to save some *pesitos* you..."

Her thoughts were crushed by her daughter Graciela, who snuck up behind her.

"Still talking to Papá, eh Mami?"

Fermina started and Cervantes sprang on top of the TV set, hackles up like the frond of a pineapple.

"*Ave María Purísima, muchacha,* one of these days you'll give me a heart attack! Look what you've done!" Fermina spread out her shaking hands for Graciela's inspection.

"Sorry, Mami." Graciela plunked down on the sofa, picked up the remote and started channel surfing. Something Fermina hated.

"Don't get carried away, Graciela. Mahreelee Cagan is on soon."

"Who?"

"Mahreelee, Mahreelee."

"Yeah, I got that, but did you say her last name was *cagan,* to shit? In the plural?"

"What a strange name, *verdad*? I'd change it if I was her. Imagine, everybody thinking her family was named after, you know, something so filthy."

"It's probably pronounced Kagan in English, you know, with the broad *a*?"

"Whatever." Fermina waved both hands in front of her face. She was nettled by any perceived criticism of her talk show idols.

Graciela made a face.

"What's the matter?" Fermina asked angrily. "Your mouth full of live fire ants or something?"

"Sorry, Mami." Graciela attempted to mollify her mother with a big kiss.

"Don't you see the shows, *m'ija*? They're so educational. You don't know how much I learn from these shows," Fermina said, appeased.

"Such as?"

"Oh, a lotta things. Like the other day, Salee Rafael had a show about men who treat women like slaves. Can you believe in this day and age that sort of thing going on? There was this man who makes his wife clean his behind after he goes to the, you know, the *servicio*."

"You mean a guy makes his wife wipe his ass? And she does it? You call that educational?"

Fermina rolled her eyes up to the ceiling beams made of ausubo wood and thought to herself, *How can this woman go to medical school and not know nothing about nothing?*

Her head bobbed and nodded.

"I learned that some men think that that is what a woman is for."

"You hadn't noticed this before?" Graciela shook her head. "Sometimes I wish you would take up calligraphy or go to the malls or something."

"Not those malls, *m'ija!!* You don't want to know what goes on in those places."

"Don't tell me. I'll pass on that one."

"Okay with me if you don't wanna learn about life. And you a doctor and all. Well, I'll get you a little coffee before you go to the hospital."

Fermina got up and, with a slight limp that favored her left leg, headed for the kitchen.

Graciela followed her to the kitchen and frowned. "Did you hurt yourself, Ma?"

"No, *m'ija*. So how's everything at the hospital?"

"Don't change the subject. What have you been up to now? Tell me the truth." Graciela's eyes narrowed with suspicion.

Fermina wouldn't look at her. Graciela took this to be a bad sign.

"Well, you know, I borrowed this tape from Mariluz's girl. She wants to be a model, you know?" Fermina limped around the kitchen bustling and clattering pots and pans.

"What's all the fuss, Ma? All you gotta do is turn on the espresso machine I gave you and put some milk in the microwave." Graciela took charge and prepared the coffee herself. "So, what kind of tape is this you borrowed? God, this is like pulling teeth!"

"Exercise, you know, for fitness," Fermina mumbled.

"Since when have you been interested in that sort of thing? I can't believe it, my own mother prancing to the tune of an exercise videotape!" Graciela paused and stared at her mother in horror.

"Wait a minute. Ma, are you by any chance, uh, how can I put this delicately...in love?" Graciela turned up her nose so high you would think she was assailed by a putrid smell.

"What, are you crazy?" It was Fermina's turn to be horrified. "I'm almost sixty-five years old, look at this head full of gray hair." She plunged her chin into her chest to show

Graciela. "And with a pack a grandchildren. None from you, by the way. I gotta foot in the grave already, what do I want with an old man?"

Graciela, much relieved, could afford to joke. "How about a *gallito,* a young rooster?"

"That's all I need, someone after my Social Security checks. No, thank you."

"So why the fitness craze all of a sudden?"

"Okay, I'll tell you, but don't blab it to Eduardo or anyone else, okay? I'm too old to be my son-in-law's laughingstock." Fermina sipped some of the strong coffee that she took *puya,* black and with no sugar.

"I still wanna be on a talk show. I know I promised you girls that I wouldn't try again." She dipped a cube of cheddar cheese in her coffee.

"Ma, what am I gonna do with you? You already tried to train those cats to do tricks, unsuccessfully, I might add. You attempted to start the first psychic telephone service in Puerto Rico and got into trouble with the Treasury Department. Then, you wanted to be the first anorexic senior citizen in history, but couldn't give up pork... or that cheese you shouldn't be eating." Fermina looked up at her daughter guiltily, but Graciela continued. "Next thing, you'll try to establish a religious cult."

"Hey, good idea."

"Forget I said that."

"But listen, Graciela, anyone can be famous today. All you need is to do something strange, like that man who had his peepee pierced on Jeree Espringel." Fermina pointed at an indistinct spot below her belly.

"Oh, my God, Ma, that's sick."

"Yeah, yeah, but they have stupid things too. Like a little kid who collects toothpaste. It was so-o-o boring. *Imagínate,* I snored all through the show. But I got an idea. If I become a senior fitness queen, you know, at my age, that's something else, *verdad*? So maybe I can get on Rolonda or Monte Güilian or my favorite of all Geraldo Rivera and show the whole United States that an old Puerto Rican woman can do exercises and look, you know, good. I'll be famous."

Graciela rolled her eyes up and sighed. "Ma, you gotta stop watching TV all day. Ever since Pa died that's all you do."

"Don't say that. You know I got other things to do, like take care of all these cats and my orchids."

Graciela glanced at her watch and got up. "Ma, I'm on duty in half an hour, so I gotta go. But I'm really worried about you. Do you want to see someone about your little problem?"

"What problem you talking about?"

"You seem to be addicted to television, Ma," Graciela said.

"Addiction? Like some drug? On the Oprah show there were some real addicts. Like the man who got addicted to those nicotine patches he bought to stop smoking and had his arms all full of them all the time."

"Okay, Ma. We'll talk about this later. By the way, did you catch the news conference that Güiche gave last night?"

"The mayor? Why waste my time? That man has nothing to say. And he's got such a nice name, José Luis Santos. It's so disrespectful to let people call him by that silly nickname he got when he was just a boy."

"It was about the *chupacabras*."

"Did they find him? I hope so," Fermina said with conviction, "because I'm afraid that thing is going to kill one of my cats any day now. You don't know how much I worry."

"It hasn't attacked cats yet, Ma. Just rabbits and dogs. And, of course, remember that the first victims were goats who had all their blood sucked out."

"Too bad it didn't suck on Don Jacinto's goats," Fermina said sadly.

"Well, you won't believe what Güiche said. Listen to this. Our mayor actually announced, on television, that the *chupacabras* isn't an animal. It's an alien from outer space. Not only that, but he organized an expedition to track it down. Can you believe it?"

"Don't look at me. I didn't vote for him."

❖ ❖ ❖

After Graciela left, Fermina had half an hour to tend to her orchids before the Maury Povich Show. Maybe she should do her weight lifting too. She didn't know whether she could keep up with this exercise business, though. It was tough. Then the lady on the exercise video said, quite emphatically, "Cut out the fat!" And Fermina knew she could not live without the pork with crackling that she loved to roast every Sunday. Or the stewed eggplants with lots of garlic, dripping in extra virgin olive oil. Or plantain fritters stuffed with crabmeat, for that matter. No, this plan wasn't going to work.

She limped to the orchid shed, mumbling to her cats, the orchids and herself.

"My *florecitas* need me now. Shoo, Teehee, out of my way. One of these days you gonna make me trip and break my neck," Fermina said to the small cat whose fur was white as coconut meat.

Humming softly, she snipped a dead leaf here and sprayed a dry plant there. "How are my pretty girls? Oh, my darlings need a little water and some food, don't you, my *preciosas?*"

She moved the plants that did not take well to a full day of sun toward the shaded corners of the shed to join those that needed to be well protected. Fermina bent down to move a large pot. She groaned and straightened up, rubbing the small of her back. As a flash of pain hit her coccyx, an idea struck her. Eagerly, she turned to Teehee.

"I got it! What if I grow the biggest, most beautiful, most fragrant orchids in the world. Can't let those damn flies fertilize them, though, they stink up all the flowers. Only bees. And I make the bees feed on my thyme bushes somehow and then I try to find a fertilizer that makes them grow and grow like Doña Marta's banana plants. She told me herself she was using this hormone to make her plants grow and they're so big. Humongous, like my grandson says. You'll see *gatita linda*, I'll be on Rolonda or Oprah or Charlee Perez. And I don't have to do those stupid exercises. It was after those *malditos* sit-ups this morning that I feel like someone ground my bones like peppercorns in a great big *pilón*."

Fermina looked down at Teehee, who had a rear paw stuck up in the air and was vigorously licking her behind.

"Is that what you think of my idea, *gata?*"

Fermina harrumphed and limped as fast as she could into the house to check the living-room clock which was just then pinging the hour. When she clicked on the TV, Maury Povich was giving a prize to a man who had the worst luck of any other contestant. The man, who won a trip to the Bahamas, all expenses paid, told the audience of his fishing accident. He jumped into a river to retrieve a fishing pole, not knowing that a signpost had been thrown and hidden in the weeds. He jumped right on the signpost and a piece of wood impaled him between the legs. He saw blood gushing all over the place, and when he touched the spot where the blood was coming from, he realized his testicles had been torn off. They sewed them back on, but he couldn't have sex now.

"*Ave María Purísima,*" Fermina said out loud as she put her hands to her head. "Can't complain about my luck, let me tell you," she addressed Ewok, who just happened to stop in front of the television to lick his front paw and then proceeded to groom his face.

"When you come right down to it," she continued while Ewok blinked in her direction and yawned, "I had a good life with my Neftalí, may he rest in peace. My daughters are good to me and always help me out whenever I need it. I have beautiful grandchildren, but I don't know when that Graciela's gonna give me some before I die. Then I have my orchids and you sweeties. Come here, Eeee-goo-ah," Fermina patted her lap and Ewok swooped into it and gave her a vigorous knead.

"*Ay*, don't dig your claws into my thigh like that!"

It was a quiet evening. Graciela was busy at the hospital and called to say she wouldn't be stopping by. Mariluz, who lived way out in San Juan, only visited on weekends. Fermina was sorry there were no talk shows on in the evening, but then she needed some time to figure out how she could grow the most impressive orchids. Maybe if she grafted an orchid plant onto an orange tree while feeding them those superduper hormones Doña Marta had. She could call the hybrid *chinorqui*. She liked that. It had a nice ring to it. She could just imagine the fragrance of an orchid fertilized by a thyme-fed bee and combined with orange blossoms. It was sure to be heavenly. She had to talk to Doña Marta tomorrow, *a primera hora*, to get her advice. She had to brace herself, she thought, because Doña Marta talked and talked and she always made Fermina feel really tired. But Doña Marta knew more than anyone, even more than Don Jacinto, about plant hormones.

"Frankly," Fermina muttered to herself, "I think she feeds those hormones to her son. He's bigger than a refrigerator.

And where did that come from? Doña Marta is tinier than a *coquí* and her husband, why he's as small as a cumin seed."

With these reflections, Fermina filled a hot skillet with pork chops. "Am I glad I don't have to do that fitness business anymore. One day was enough for me!"

Just as she was turning a pork chop with a long two-tined fork, Fermina heard a loud bang in the orchid shed. Fork in hand, she stepped over the cats, who were hungrily collected around the stove—even Bruno, the nervous one, was there. She tiptoed to the door and very quietly went into the dark shed. The noise came from the potting area. At first, she heard a sound like crumpled paper tossed by the wind against a wall. Then she could hear the metallic clatter of gardening tools and buckets. For a moment, Fermina thought it was an earthquake. But then, through the slant of light coming from the kitchen, she saw a short, stubby tail. She reared up her head as though someone had poured vinegar up her nose when she realized that, mingled with the sweet scent of her orchids, there was the unmistakable stench of male goat in rut. As she crept to the potting table, she caught sight of mangled flowers and bruised leaves on the ground. To Fermina's horror, the goat was poking a basket of tiny seedlings and munching at the contents contentedly.

"You son of an old goat, you," Fermina seethed. She jumped, fork in hand, toward the animal. Too startled to leap out of harm's way—Fermina's way, that is—the goat stood, transfixed with fear for a split second before reacting. Fermina poked him in the neck with her sturdy cooking fork.

The goat bucked wildly and, when it flung its head back, disengaged the fork from his neck. He stumbled out of the shed, leaving a trail of broken pots, torn petals and strewn dirt in his wake. Fermina clutched her bloodied fork like a trident and hurled invectives at the beast.

"You devil, you demon, look what you've done. And that Don Jacinto who smells like an old goat himself! Wish I could get my hands on that fool right now."

She flicked on the light switch and gently picked up her seedlings.

"My little sweeties. Destroyed. Completely." She held the tiny crumbled plants in her palm and pressed them to her chest, her face set angrily.

"I hope the damn goat is dead. Where's that good-for-nothing *chupacabras* when you need him? I tell you, Cervantes, what is this world coming to when they let ugly, filthy goats trample all over the most beautiful, the most delicate flowers in the world? There is no justice in this world. No justice at all."

❖ ❖ ❖

That evening Don Jacinto, inevitably, paid Fermina a visit. Fermina would have loved to pierce his neck with a fork too, but she had to be civil. Too bad.

Don Jacinto's permanent scowl was deeper, darker, when he entered the living room. Fermina turned off the TV and bid him to sit down.

"May I get you some coffee or maybe a glass of lemonade, Don Jacinto?"

He looked at the chair before sitting down, as though expecting nettles to have been placed there for his discomfort.

"One of my billy goats was hurt," he charged into the discussion like a bull in a ring, without preamble. "Did you see anyone around here who may have committed such a despicable act?"

His attitude struck Fermina as very impolite. He could have at least inquired about her health, her family, talked about the weather, and then settled into this business with the goat.

"And how is Doña Martina?" She was determined to display some common courtesy even though the injured party in this business was certainly her.

"The billy goat, that's what I want to talk about. I'm a busy man, so don't waste my time. My goat was stabbed," he stated curtly.

"Is he dead?" Fermina asked hopefully.

"Injured. Two vampire-like punctures in the neck. Whoever did this had fangs, I'm sure of it." His eyebrows almost touched his hairline.

"Well, I have told you a million times that your goats are always jumping into my *finca*, destroying my beautiful orchids. Why don't you keep those smelly goats on your own property where they belong?"

"Give me a break! Those flowers of yours aren't worth my goats' *caca!*"

"*Perdón*. Pardon me?"

"Listen, Doña Fermina, I'm a reasonable man."

Fermina snorted.

Don Jacinto's dark bushy eyebrows came together and he dropped his voice. "Was it by any chance you who inflicted the wounds on my billy goat? If so, you pay me the vet expenses, promise you'll never hurt one of my animals again, and I won't report you. Don't forget, the mayor is my son's best friend and *compadre*. If I report you, Güiche's office is involved and it could become a big scandal. Now, is that what you want?"

"How dare you come into my own home and accuse me of something like that?" Fermina threw her head back. "I want you to get out of my house this minute!"

"You crazy old woman. You belong in the loony bin."

"*Viejo sinvergüenza*," Fermina cried after Don Jacinto stalked off. "I bet he's on his way to the police right now. Or worse, running with his tail between his legs to that stupid mayor we have. May his tongue fall off before he starts spreading tales about me through the whole town. Maybe I'll be lucky and the mayor is out hunting the *chupacabras* tonight."

Fermina was too upset to watch her favorite soap opera or even call her daughters. She burned with rage and rocked vigorously in her chair while she mumbled to herself.

"Should not have let my anger blind me like that. The poor goat. I hope he's okay. But what am I going to do if the police come looking for me? I gotta make something up, some kind of tale. I hope nobody saw me. *Ay, Virgen María,* help me come up with a good story to save my skin. That *viejo* don Jacinto is capable of suing me for all I've got. I could lose the farm. Everything. What can I do, what can I possibly do?" Fermina addressed all the cats who were lying about the living room, except for Bruno who, when Don Jacinto stomped into the house, had scurried away to hide, uttering squeals of distress.

Fermina was not surprised when she heard the rap on her screen door. She peeked through the curtains and saw the two young policemen. She recognized them right away. Pablito Sánchez and Chucho Jiménez. Neftalí used to thwack them with a switch when the boys played hooky and came into their *finca* to steal the plentiful Spanish limes that grow all over their property. Now they were grown men and here they are, Fermina thought, ready to cart me off to jail. I told Neftalí he shouldn't go after those kids. Those were just boyish pranks. Oh, well, I better open the door and face the music. With this uncomfortable thought, Fermina opened the screen door.

"*¿Cómo está?* How are you, Doña Fermina?" Chucho inquired politely as he and Pablito came in.

Fermina shooed Greta so the young men could occupy the sofa. After some preliminary conversation about the weather, their families and the state of the crops, Pablito cleared his throat.

"Sorry to bother you at this time of night, Doña Fermina, but the mayor's office called us."

"Would you like some *cafecito,* my sons?" Fermina interrupted.

"No, *gracias,*" Pablito continued while Chucho bent down to pet Teehee who, not knowing this was inappropriate behavior toward an upholder of the law, had been purring and rubbing against his leg.

"So, what can I do for you?"

"A goat belonging to Don Jacinto was stabbed this evening," Pablito said. "He filed a complaint against you. He seems to think you may have had something to do with the incident."

"No, *m'ijo,* I was cooking for all these cats. You don't know how much they eat. And all they want is meat with rice and beans. Just like people. Then, I had my dinner too, we all eat together, you know, and then, let me see," Fermina searched for inspiration in the ceiling beams, "I watched television—the eight o'clock soap opera was on. And now, my goodness, look at the time it is, I was getting ready to go to bed. I gotta lot of things to do tomorrow. Before the first rooster crows, I gotta get up, *imagínense.*"

Chucho straightened up. "Doña Fermina, did you see or hear anything suspicious while you were cooking, or having dinner, or watching television?"

Ay Dios mío, these kids were interrogating her, Fermina Beltrán, who had lived a blameless life. That her head full of gray hairs should have to bear this shame! And all because of that *viejo* Don Jacinto. Forget about a lawsuit, he wanted her in jail, that's what the old goat wanted.

"To tell you the truth, I did see something." Fermina paused for effect and to collect her scattered thoughts. "I was cooking when I saw one of Don Jacinto's goats in my orchid shed. So I went out wiping my hands on the apron. You see, just then I had one eye on the skillet and the other on those cats, they're such grubbos, especially that Eee-goo-ah, he's perfectly capable of jumping into the pan to snatch one of the pork chops. Anyway, where was I? Oh, yes. I stamped on the floor and shooed the goat away. Then," Fermina paused to let some breath out and inhale again, "suddenly I saw this flash of light, red light, yes, that was it, red light, maybe it had a little blue in it too, and, and this thing, this big flying thing came down from the heavens, like, like a ball of fire and the next thing I knew the ball of fire was on the poor goat. The goat was running like the devil who just saw the cross, but the thing was kind of stuck to his neck."

Fermina reached for her own neck while she searched in the policemen's expressions to see what effect her startling revelation had had on them. Pablito and Chucho looked at each other and did not say a word. Fermina, in her nervousness, decided to plunge ahead. She had never lied like this before, but it was easy, she thought. In fact, the more she lied, the easier it got, especially if she talked fast.

"So there I am, *imagínense,* worried about the poor goat, *bendito,* but I had to run into the house because I could smell the pork chops burning." Fermina stared at the policemen pie-eyed, trying to look as innocent as the *Virgen María.* She nodded a few times and then shook her head to express the amazement her experience had instilled in her.

"Um, Doña Fermina, why didn't you inform Don Jacinto of this when he came to see you?" Chucho asked.

"That's a very good question, young man! You boys are so smart, I'm so happy you turned out okay after playing hooky so much, remember?"

The minute she said that, Fermina clamped her mouth shut. *Caramba,* shouldn't have mentioned that, she thought, after Neftalí clobbered them so soundly.

"I'm sorry my late husband, may he rest in peace, went after you, you know, because of the limes, but he was a nervous man and sometimes his temper got the best of him."

"That was a long time ago, Doña Fermina, don't worry about that," Pablito said. "But could you answer the question, please?"

"What question was that, *m'ijito?*"

"Why didn't you inform Don Jacinto about this fireball, or whatever it was."

Fermina crossed her arms over her chest angrily. "That *maleducado* dared to come into my very own home and insult me. In my very own home. *¡Qué falta de respeto!* How disrespectful! He takes advantage of me because I'm just an old widow, who has no one to defend her. I don't even have any sons. Your mothers are lucky to have you two. Look at you, so handsome in those uniforms. Your mothers must be very, very proud."

Fermina, who loved her daughters fiercely and never cared to have sons at all, pretended to wipe an errant tear with her thumb.

"Calm down, Doña Fermina," Chucho said. "Your statement is very important. You know the mayor is collecting information on *chupacabras* sightings. He thinks it's an extraterrestrial being. Didn't you see him on television making the announcement? Maybe that's what you saw, the *chupacabras,*" he added.

"Sí, sí, eso mismo, that's it!" Fermia replied enthusiastically. This was turning out better than she thought. "The *chupacabras,* imagine that."

"Last night, the *chupacabras* struck again," Pablito said. "It mutilated two sheep down in El Tuque."

"Did it suck all their blood out?" Fermina might as well find out as much as she could about this *chupacabras*.

"We don't have the details right now. But we do know that Don Jacinto's goat was injured. We checked him out ourselves. Lucky for him that the goat's still alive. It was a close call."

"Oh, yes, that was lucky," Fermina said without enthusiasm.

"We won't bother you anymore tonight, but tomorrow morning we'll pick you up at around nine to take you to the station. Then we can fill out a complete report of the sighting. For the mayor's office, you understand. Is that convenient for you, Doña Fermina?" Pablito said politely as he and Chucho got up to leave.

"You gonna arrest me? I didn't do nothing." Fermina's heart sank when she thought they had caught on to her lies. She shot a desperate glance at the telephone. She had to call Mariluz and Graciela.

Chucho patted Fermina on the shoulder. "No, Doña Fermina, we'll explain everything to Don Jacinto right now. Don't worry, no one will arrest you. We just need a report for the mayor. He's a friend of Don Jacinto's family, you see." And he winked at Fermina.

News of the *chupacabras* sighting by Fermina Beltrán spread like wildfire throughout the island. From San Juan to Ponce to Mayagüez, reporters from newspapers, radio stations and even TV rushed to Barrio Esperanza in Canóvanas to interview Fermina. A photograph of her sitting stiffly in her rocking chair and surrounded by all her cats (except Bruno, who, true to his nature, quivered under the bed), appeared in *El Nuevo Día, The San Juan Star* and even in *El Vocero*.

In the midst of a press conference held at Güiche's office, Graciela elbowed her way through the throng and pulled Fermina to the side.

"Ma, let me get you an appointment with a psychiatrist."

"You think I'm crazy?" Fermina whispered and grabbed Graciela's arm. "Come to the house, so I can tell you what happened."

Over several cups of coffee and lots of cubed cheddar cheese, Fermina recounted the story of her imminent arrest and destitution at the merciless hands of the hideous Don Jacinto. Just as Fermina was about to ask Graciela's advice on what to do with this mess, the phone rang.

"The phone always rings when you're busy," Fermina muttered.

"Hello, who is it calling?" Fermina had an uneasy alliance with the phone.

"Yes, I am Fermina Beltrán, *a sus órdenes*. Who? Is this true? I cannot believe it! Yes, I can go there. Anytime you want. Okay, whatever you say. Thank you, thank you, *señor* Geraldo."

With a smile broader than the side of her house, Fermina hung up the phone.

The Wound[1]

Tenerías is a place deep in Ponce where wounds never heal. Laura had heard the legend of Tenerías many times in her childhood. Anyone injured there either died or was plagued with the unrelenting pain of an unhealed wound.

Laura tried to wipe her own wound from the mirror that stared back at her and rubbed her eyes until they stung. She was old and the colors in her mind had faded. She no longer remembered the tints of tropical light that flushed her cheeks when the sun was about to set, and a pearly translucence sharpened her senses. What color was it? Was the light of her childhood white or yellow or blue? She could not say. Somehow her mind erased what she wanted to remember, yet recalled with great precision what she would rather forget.

But the wound of Tenerías was not really in her memory. It was somewhere deeper than memory could ever be.

She looked out the window of her second-floor apartment. San Sebastián Street was quiet. It was siesta time in Old San Juan. The shops closed and shuttered for the several hours

---

[1]Editorial note: This story is based on a historical event called the Ponce Massacre, which occurred in Puerto Rico in 1937 when the police, under orders from Governor Winship, opened fire on an unarmed crowd and twenty-one persons were killed and over 150 injured.

the sun was at its hottest. People dropped off like flies after lunch. The sun was sharp indeed, but Laura shivered, pulled her shutters in, and sank into the comfort of darkness. Swaying in her wicker rocking chair, she listened to her neighbor's radio. *Amor de mis amores,* a male voice crooned longingly.

Love. She could not recall even that. Perhaps love has no color and that is why it lingers at the edge of her voice and she cannot remember how to call it. For surely, calling it love, alone, would not do. Love was coupled with hurt. Like that awful hurt in Ponce so many years back, so far back, yet it felt as fused to her as flesh.

II

Laura was born in 1927, in the town of Camuy. Though those were hard times in Puerto Rico, Laura remembered how happy their lives had been then. Warmed by the bright morning sunshine, she and her mother Elpidia set off with wide wicker baskets to the tobacco fields at harvest time. As her mother worked, Laura would skip happily to the riverbank, hiking up her skirt. She giggled to herself and threw pebbles into the water just to hear them plop. In her unique conversations with the river, she would watch the endless circles rippling away from each other and she would attempt to decipher the river's message to her. Then, believing herself loved by the river, she would twirl and sway like Nausikaa, the sea-loving princess she had read about in school.

"Laura," her mother would yell holding up a bunch of tobacco leaves. "Get back here this minute, *muchacha!* One day you're going to slip and fall into the river."

Laura would then retreat as long as Elpidia watched closely with her thick black eyebrows knit in a tight seam. But as soon as she saw her mother's white kerchief bend over the field and her ear tilt toward the gossiping women who worked beside her, she wended her way back to the riverbank.

Laura knew the river's moods like a lover's. On clear days, it glimmered, happily thrusting sunshine from its blue surface. When it rained, the deep gray waters saddened her and she found it hard to look into its depths. On those days, she got drenched while she ran toward the river. Midway there, she turned around and walked clumsily backwards until she could sense she was close to the water. Then she closed her eyes and tossed stones over her head until she heard them plop. Reassured that the river still spoke to her in the language they both understood, Laura ran home to face the scolding her grandmother Socorro always had in store for her when she played outside in the rain.

The family lived in a small wooden house that remained dry and cozy even during the rainy season. The walls were covered with family portraits and gilt-framed renderings of the Sacred Heart of Jesus, the Virgin Mary and Saint Gabriel Archangel, and had mirrors half set into the wall. Every evening Laura would lie by the light of a beeswax candle and examine the wooden ceiling. Her father had painted a huge golden star on the ceiling and it sparkled in the dark. She spent hours there during her childhood, imagining the universe the teacher talked about in school, big and dark and mysterious, hovering like a mist over her upturned face.

While contemplating the universe, Laura listened to her mother humming as she settled down after the household chores to do her embroidery. Elpidia waited up for her husband as long as she could bear without nodding off. Claudio was either away cutting cane at whatever plantations offered work or seemed to be engaged in activities Laura knew very little about. On many evenings, Elpidia was alone with Laura, her first child, and her mother, Socorro. Of the four infants born to Elpidia, only Laura had lived.

Finding work as a cutter was hard after the sugar workers' strike, but Claudio was strong, hardworking and willing to travel great distances for a job. At daybreak, Claudio usually donned his straw hat, hefted the machete he kept leaning against the wall, and headed toward the cane fields. He cut cane during the harvest and labored at other plantation chores during the so-called *tiempo muerto* or dead season. When the cane fields were littered with stubble after the harvest, he joined a throng of men to burn and clear the fields of trash and termites, spread new seeds and dig irrigation ditches. He mended palisades, repaired thatched roofs, and patched burlap sacks. He worked from sunrise to sunset.

On the evenings when he was home, Claudio sat in a rocker on the small balcony by the light of kerosene lamps, called *quinqués*. He sucked deeply on his cigarette and contemplated the darkness. Laura always wondered what he thought about after dinner as he sat alone, smoking and thinking.

Laura remembered the evening when she had been so happy to have her father home and her godfather Luis came to their house while the family sat at the table having thick cassava soup. Luis gave Laura his blessing and turned to Claudio.

"Can we count on your help for the parade, *compadre?*" Luis asked as Elpidia served him a bowl of soup.

"You know I'm available for anything the party needs." He waited for Luis to sit down.

"When is it?" Claudio asked.

"Palm Sunday."

"We still have a few months to get ready, but there's a lot of organizing to do, not just for the parade, but for the general party meeting afterwards."

"Did we get official permission, finally?"

"Oh, sure," Luis said easily. "We really don't need authorization, but we requested permission from the mayor of Ponce as a courtesy. He said yes."

"What else could he do? He knows that parades organized by the Nationalists are a lot of fun. People love them," Claudio said.

"That's right, he's just being a good politician. That means a popular one in his book."

After dinner, Claudio brought out a bottle of *ron cañita* from the cupboard, put an arm around his friend's shoulders, and led him to the balcony. The evening was cool and moist. It had rained earlier and the *coquís* sang noisily. The men sat on the balcony rail whispering and drinking for over an hour.

Laura helped Elpidia and Socorro wash up the dinner dishes in a basin of rainwater and stack them to dry. She noticed how Elpidia would frequently turn to the men's voices and her face blanched with anxiety. When Luis left, Elpidia stood under the lintel, her figure heavy with child cut against the outside darkness, watching him disappear into the night.

It distressed Elpidia that Claudio was called for party duties again. The situation was getting more difficult for members of the party after the arrest of many of its leaders. She concealed her fear as best she could, but Laura saw how her mouth stitched grimly. Elpidia was trembling when Laura tugged at her skirt. She pulled the girl against her swollen belly. But Elpidia knew what was expected of her. As quickly as her advanced stage would allow, Elpidia wrapped some dry meat and bread in a clean handkerchief. Claudio kissed little Laura on the head and his wife and mother-in-law on both cheeks and slipped into the night. Laura peered into the starlit night, searching for him in the darkness, as he walked away.

The next morning Elpidia loaded the stove with kindling for their morning coffee. Laura was setting gourd cups on the table when she noticed her mother staring at the puddle that collected at her feet. Elpidia was sweating, though it was cool in the kitchen.

"Hurry," she said, "call *Abuela*."

Laura rushed out to the garden where her *abuela* Socorro was spreading laundered sheets on lavender bushes. When they went into the house, Elpidia was in bed fully dressed, her thick black hair tightly plaited. Laura had rarely seen her mother lying down during the daytime. It all seemed amiss: her bulging abdomen under the apron, the sweat that washed over her, her groans, her ashen lips.

"Go outside," *Abuela* ordered, "and make yourself useful."

Useful? Laura asked herself. What in the world could she do, but sob at the obvious demise of her dear mother? Time did not count for much in her childhood, but that morning, punctuated by moans and grunts, was one of the longest of her short life.

The sun was dropping when Laura heard a sharp slap and a wail coming from her parents' tiny bedroom. Laura rushed in and saw a baby crying lustily while Socorro bundled it up in cotton swaddling. Elpidia unbuttoned her blouse and put a large dark nipple into the baby's mouth. It sucked hungrily for a while and fell asleep. Laura stood at the foot of the bed staring at her exhausted mother with the tiny, blood-red baby at her breast. Elpidia noticed the girl's gaping mouth and beckoned her to approach.

"Laura," she said, "you have a little brother now. His name's Pedro."

Laura couldn't find anything to say.

"What's the matter, *nena?*" Elpidia asked her.

"Can I touch him?" Laura said timidly.

Elpidia took Laura's hand and placed it gently on the baby's cheek. It was so soft and velvety, Laura found it hard to take her hand away.

"You can kiss him too, if you want," Socorro said while she tidied up the birth mess.

Laura gave Pedro the first of the many kisses she would later dispense on his head, neck, cheeks, and hands. His little head was soft, tender and scented. He smelled like freshly cut wood and warm milk.

News of the birth traveled like brushfire and, through a cord of messengers, reached Claudio at a remote sugar plantation where he had been working. Toward the end of that week, late in the night it must have been, for they were all asleep, including Socorro, who tended to be an insomniac, they heard the floorboards creak as someone snuck into the house. Elpidia, whose sleep was very light after years of having dead babies, padded to the kitchen. Laura pretended to sleep, but was wide awake because little Pedro had been crying for his feeding and she had not yet drifted back to her dreams. She saw Claudio's dark figure in the bedroom. Quietly following Elpidia, who held a lighted candle, he approached the sleeping infant. Laura would never forget it.

He took the baby in his arms and in the yellow pool of candle light, he whispered very gently, "Now that you've come into the world, I must leave."

Such a long time and to think she remembered. At times she could not remember the events of the current week, yet the past of her childhood was vivid in her mind. If only she could go out and clear her head, distract herself with the sights of sidewalk ice cream vendors, fashionable boutiques, kiosks selling newspapers and magazines from all over the world. But Laura rarely ventured out of her small apartment. She was afraid of being trapped by the multitudes in buses and swallowed by the crowds buzzing through the hard cobblestoned streets. She sat on the porch when the worst heat of the sun had waned and looked down at the busy people coming and going like swarms of bees feeding on thyme bushes. A heaviness and shortness of breath overcame her and she rushed inside to sit on her rocker and gather her thoughts around her like a shawl until it was time to feed the cat.

III

Little Laura begged Claudio to take her to the Nationalist Palm Sunday parade. Everyone in Camuy was talking about it, making plans to go all the way to Ponce to attend. It was so much fun to watch Nationalist men and women marching to band music, spectators laughing and singing and waving flags. And there would be lots of kiosks lining the streets selling *piraguas,* chips scraped from huge chunks of ice, fitted like pyramids into paper cones and soaked in thick fruity syrups. Vendors would also hawk tasty snacks and sweet cool drinks from ice chests. Her father, she was sure, would give her some *chavitos* to spend and Laura would feel like a grownup.

"What do you think, Elpidia? You want me to take *la nena?*" Claudio sat Laura on his lap and stroked her hair.

Elpidia put down her embroidery. "I wish the baby wasn't so small and I could go too. But I worry about *la nena.* She's only ten. Who's going to keep an eye on her? You'll be busy with other things, won't you?"

Laura sat in her father's lap, hugging him around the neck, and dared not say a word. She held her breath waiting for her fate to be discussed and determined.

"Everything's pretty well organized by now," Claudio said. "Besides, Luis' wife, our *comadre* Ana, is going. She can look after Laura while I'm busy."

When Elpidia sighed and shrugged her shoulders, Laura knew she would give in. By the time Elpidia responded, Laura was grinning broadly.

"Oh, all right, but only if Ana agrees to look after her. I'll have a talk with her myself."

❖ ❖ ❖

Palm Sunday was on March 21. The year was 1937. Laura had written it down in her notebook just before Easter vacation while Mr. Johnson, her American teacher, droned on about the American Revolution.

Elpidia had taught Laura to read and write in Spanish at home. In the schools they were only allowed to teach and speak in English. Luckily, Mr. Johnson had just arrived in Puerto Rico and did not speak a word of Spanish, so Laura felt she had a secret language she could communicate in with her friends at school and in her notebook.

She had to be careful not to be caught by her teacher, though. She would be punished with ruler blows on her palms or having to write "I will not write in Spanish" a hundred times on the chalkboard. Mr. Johnson had a smooth, bare pate and his baldness stretched past the dome of his head. Only a narrow strip of blond hair rimmed the back of his head. He always wore a shirt and tie, something the children found strange, especially since he never seemed to perspire. His hands were big and strong, and he could easily grasp children who attempted to run away from his punishments.

Whenever Mr. Johnson had to leave the room, he would order the children not to speak Spanish or they would be punished severely. Then, he would perform an act that horrified them all into silence. He would bring out a brandy glass from his desk drawer and place it on top of the desk. Next, he would grope around in his eye socket with a thumb and forefinger and pluck out a glass eye. Slowly, deliberately, he would raise his arm to show the blue glass eye, shiny and hard and hair-raising, to the stunned class. Then, he would plunk the eye into the brandy glass.

"I'm leaving for a few minutes," he would say solemnly. "But my eye stays here to watch you while I'm gone. If any of you starts speaking Spanish, even one word, the eye will know who it is and, when I put it back in, I will know too."

The children couldn't understand the words, but they understood the malice in the teacher's voice, the frenzy of his gestures.

So Laura's heart pounded when she wrote the date of the Palm Sunday parade in the back of her notebook, while Mr. Johnson's back was turned toward the chalkboard. Laura did not need a reminder of that important date and event. But writing it down made it more real to her and increased her anticipation.

※ ※ ※

On Palm Sunday, Laura was too excited to have breakfast. A group of *Camueños* and people from surrounding towns met at the plaza to join the cavalcade of buses and automobiles that would wind up and down the mountains of the Cordillera Central, climbing up from the northern city of Arecibo and coasting down to the southern coastal city of Ponce. It was a long trip and they were forced to start out before daybreak.

Ana gripped Laura's hand tightly when they boarded the bus and they took a seat by a window. Days before, her husband, Luis, had gone ahead to Ponce with Claudio and the other party organizers.

Laura had never taken such a long trip and was impatient to get going. She felt a pang of guilt when she remembered that her mother had to stay home nursing little Pedro and Socorro had decided to keep her company. She fidgeted until she couldn't sit still any longer and stood up from her seat to peer at the other passengers who were boarding and carrying on noisy and lengthy discussions about who would sit where and with whom. Whole families boarded the bus—children, parents, grandparents. Everyone in Camuy seemed to be headed for the parade.

"Sit down and be still, *niña!*" Ana ordered with a severe look. Ana was slim and pretty and wore her long brown hair in a bun. She was young, but strong-willed and short-tempered.

Laura obeyed her without question. Laura sat quietly and smoothed the folds of the new blue dress her grandmother had sewn. It was the only nice dress she owned, and she would wear it for all special occasions until she grew out of it. She had promised *Abuela* she would take care not to soil it today, so she could wear it again for Easter Mass. By the time the bus pulled out, it was already six and the early morning dew was drifting through the shreds of light.

The steep road was full of treacherous curves, and the bus had to climb the road slowly, honking before each turn. Some of the hairpin curves were marked with white crosses in memory of people who had died in accidents at those spots. The feathery leaves of flamboyant trees shimmered in the bright sun as the bus climbed higher and deeper into the mountains. Laura had plenty of time to sit back, feel the cool mountain breeze on her face, and enjoy the scenery.

The screeching brakes awoke Laura from a short doze, and she realized they were now rolling down from the mountains, bus under tight control, toward the southern coast. Once on the flatland, she felt a blast of heat. Acres of sugarcane swayed under the scorching sun, the blond spears humbled by the weight of the thick humid air. At a distance, smoke puffs smudged the blue horizon. The odor of burned earth and charred stalks made Laura's empty stomach turn.

She wished she had eaten after all, and wondered whether her *madrina* had brought anything to munch on. Her hunger pangs got worse when she saw the local peons, machetes at their sides, resting under the shade of the black laurels that lined the roads, having their morning coffee with chunks of water bread.

The early morning light swept the dawn coolness aside and, swollen with humidity, cast its heat everywhere. Into sharp corners, through gaping pores, in the restless dust, the silent heat searched relentlessly. The bus passengers fanned themselves with pieces of cardboard and folded paper. Ana had come prepared for the trip with a handbag full of bread, cheese, and a thermos with sweet lemonade. She dug into her capacious bag and handed Laura a paper fan while keeping one for herself.

"Hungry, aren't you?" she asked when she noticed how avidly Laura stared at the contents of her bag.

"I was saving this for later, but you can have a snack now."

Laura chewed on some bread and lazily looked out to a landscape that was changing drastically as they approached the coast. Wooden houses and thatched huts or *bohíos* crowded together in thick patches on the flat arid land. Laura was admiring the bustling port, when her attention was captured by the sight of the city of Ponce shimmering in the noon light. It dazzled her with its immense white plaza and cathedral.

IV

Marina and Aurora Streets teemed with people of all ages. That bright Palm Sunday morning, the sun towered over the Ponce plaza, and light bounced from the glittering asphalt.

Automobiles shone like pots of oil. Puerto Rican flags and Nationalist Party ensigns flapped against tall masts. Laura searched through the throng with anticipation. She spotted her father approaching her briskly. He swept off his wide straw hat and spread out his arms like wings. Laura ran easily into his strong embrace.

"How was the ride?" he asked.

Ana put a hand on her forehead to shield her eyes from the sun when she looked up at Claudio.

"Bumpy, but okay. I was a little sick to my stomach with all those curves, but this one," she pointed her chin at Laura, "even had a snack on the way."

Claudio put Laura down, and she tried to push through the crowd, craning her neck so she could see what was happening during the parade formation. Ana pulled her back.

"Where's Luis?" she asked Claudio as she held Laura's hand in a tight grasp.

"He's finishing up some things at the club for the party meeting tonight."

"When does it start?"

"At twelve, *en punto,* on the dot. We have to maintain strict discipline now more than ever."

"That's right. Can't give them any excuse to throw more of us in jail."

"When they want an excuse, they just make it up," Claudio shrugged and strode toward the Nationalist Club.

Ana stuck her pointy elbows out and charged through the teeming spectators to the edge of the sidewalk, where she and Laura had an unhindered view. People slipped through the lines set up by the police to cordon off the area and waited eagerly for the parade to begin. Many spectators came right after the late-morning Mass, still in their Sunday finery and holding the palm fronds that had been blessed and given out to them by the priest that morning in commemoration of

Christ's arrival in Jerusalem. House balconies were packed with people waiting for the festivities to begin. People stood on automobile hoods and wooden crates. They sat high up on horses and donkeys.

Laura watched with excitement as the marchers, about one hundred men and women, began to congregate on Marina Street. The cadets wore immaculate white pants and the black shirts that, Ana explained, represented mourning for the colonial bondage of the island. The women wore white uniforms and caps. A band of four musicians milled around, tuning their instruments.

The laughter and high voices of excited people permeated the plaza. The exhilaration was contagious and Laura found herself giving little leaps into the air and giggling. Ana was trying to rein her in, when suddenly she let go of Laura's hand and put her hands to her face. Laura cringed when, after a loud drumroll, she felt a shift in the mood of the crowd. The laughter and bantering tones dissipated. Instead, a silent pall, edged with fear, settled on the crowd. Even the birds stopped chirping.

People watched nervously as hundreds of policemen fanned out into the area where the parade would take place. The policemen took their positions surrounding the crowd and stood at attention. They were armed with truncheons, rifles, submachine guns, carbines, tear gas bombs, hand grenades and revolvers. The spectators were hemmed in, cornered. They were trapped.

In the meantime, the parade commander, after surveying the situation, ordered the cadets to line up to march in columns of three deep. The women in white were already behind the cadets and, at their rear, the band began to play the national anthem, *La Borinqueña*. The marchers stood at attention, faces gleaming under the hot afternoon sun. For the few minutes during which the anthem played, the crowd forgot the presence of the police and sang with vigor. When the music stopped, the men and women began their scheduled march down Marina Street. As they approached the plaza, a police officer ordered them to halt. The marchers obeyed and stood silently, hands by their sides, except for the flag bearer who held the Puerto Rican flag high in the air.

That's when Laura heard the first shots.

Laura, her face stretched back in terror, swiveled and saw that the policemen had drawn out their weapons and were pushing toward Aurora Street, thrusting steadily ahead into the plaza. When they hit the plaza, without warning, they opened fire on the Nationalist marchers first and within seconds they were shooting at everyone in the crowd, marchers and bystanders alike. As in a dream, Laura saw the cadets still standing in silence, motionless, hands hanging at their sides. In front of them, their commander had crumpled to the ground, his body ripped apart. At the edge of the sidewalk near the marchers stood two young boys. Laura saw them as in a still photograph. One had a skinny arm around the other boy's shoulders and they stood woodenly with eyes wide open in shock and confusion. By the time the boys reacted and began to run, volleys of bullets pelted like hail from all around the plaza, injuring, maiming, killing, as people screamed and ran waving their arms, trying to fend off the horror. Minutes later, one of the boys was on the ground. A hole, red and blackened by burning pieces of shrapnel and the size of a man's fist, flared in the back of his shirt.

The day was streaked with threads of blood and sun. Women, men, and children groped their way to the surface amid clouds of smoke. They bolted in every direction to escape the shots that whistled through the air and past them. The air was thick with the sickly smell of tear gas, the hard stench of lead, and clouds of somber smoke. Corralled and slaughtered like animals, the police's prey had nowhere to go.

The well-armed hunters fired recklessly while plowing into the crowd. Scrambling with Ana for shelter, Laura was blinded by the tear gas, eyes watering, stinging. She fell and Ana dragged her to her feet. They searched with maddened eyes for a refuge that would protect them from the terrible siege. Laura's temples throbbed violently as she slipped into a daze. Each time a shot rang out, her stomach quaked. Her ears rang painfully. She wanted to crawl out of the din, make time start again so this nightmare would be over. Instead, her heart slammed like a shutter in the wind. She ran and ran by Ana's side and pressed a hand hard against her mouth.

People hid inside houses, under automobiles, behind fences. Terrified mothers held small children to their breasts and turned their backs against the bullets. The submachine gun squad bore into the crowd in a roar of fire. Cries of terror and pain tore through the air. The screams cut into the crowds' collective memory forever. The screams and shots merged into deep dark thunder, the color of midnight. The echo repeated itself, tolling like a bell, over and over, and turned into the color of madness. Laura would never forget the hellish spectacle of tin-roofed homes in flames, the mangled bodies and the streets choked with the hunted as they fled.

Madness, madness all around. And there was nowhere to go.

Laura and Ana huddled in a corner shrinking into themselves to become as small as possible. Ana shoved Laura behind her. The girl peeked around Ana's shoulder and saw the flag bearer dragging himself to the sidewalk, bleeding from holes all over his body. Laura wondered how he could still be alive. He slid down and reclined against the wall of a house, his face a clump of ash. He dipped his finger in a chest wound and, with his own blood, wrote on the wall.

"What is he doing?" Ana yelled before the flag bearer collapsed.

Laura tried to scramble out from behind Ana to see better, but the woman pushed her back.

"Stay right here, I'll go see what it is."

Ana made sure Laura was safe behind a fence and approached the fallen man. Her voice rang clearly over the pandemonium that surrounded her. She read his scribbled words, still dripping with fresh blood.

"Long live the Republic! Down with the assassins!"

Ana crawled to the dead man's side and tried to rescue the flag from the dirty pavement where it had collapsed in a pile. Just as she grabbed the flag, a policeman turned his submachine gun toward her. Laura screamed when she saw Ana fall like a broken doll with ugly holes in her dress.

The policeman forged ahead aiming wildly at another target and Laura ran out of her shelter. She clawed desperately at Ana's breast, but her *madrina* lay in a pool of blood and her eyes stared at a distance Laura knew she could not reach. Laura sobbed and pulled at Ana's arm. She pinched her cheeks and shook her. Laura looked down at her blue dress streaked with dirt and blood.

Suddenly, a small girl darted out of the smoky confusion, picked up the flag from the pavement where Ana had dropped it, and ran off, flag waving in her lifted hand. Bullets hurtled around her as she ran away from the plaza into the safety of the narrow streets.

Chaos surrounded Laura as she tried to waken Ana, looking up beseechingly, trying to identify a familiar face among the terrified people who scattered in all directions around her, fleeing from the carnage.

"Papi," she called into the crowd. "I want to go home," she sobbed.

She collapsed, whimpering like a sick puppy over her *madrina*'s fallen body. Broken bodies stretched out like a field of wild poppies around her. The plaza was drenched with the flow of blood.

V

For days Elpidia stood squeezing Laura's small hand, waiting for the ferries to arrive. The briny wind lashed their skirts during the long days they spent peering into the haunted faces of men as they clambered down the planks in single file. They were gaunt and stooped, still battling the tropical gales when they disembarked. Deep hollows cut into their faces as they squinted at the Caribbean sun. Laura's heart skipped when a tall, black-haired man with a scraggly beard faced them. She winced but held her tongue.

"Elpidia!" the man shouted and waved at her mother. The girl looked down quickly when she did not recognize his voice. Her mother wept by her side.

"Elpidia, don't you recognize me?" The tall man dropped a cardboard suitcase on the pier. The disconcerted shoes of many men shuffled by them.

"Is that you, Luis?" She clung to his frayed *guayabera*.

"*Sí, soy yo.*"

"Tell me, for God's sake, where's Claudio? You must know. Someone has to know."

He put an arm over Elpidia's shoulders and bent down to kiss little Laura's head. They walked down the road leading into the old city. The early afternoon sun rubbed their skin raw. They sat under a tree. Pinecones crackled and exploded in the dry heat.

"Claudio was wounded in Tenerías," Luis said.

That was when they knew they would never see him again. Laura unclasped her embroidered purse, turned it inside out, and counted the uncut threads in its seam and then counted them again and again because she did not know what else to do.

Elpidia wiped her face with the back of her hand, stuck her chin forward, and looked up at the emaciated man Luis had become.

"We didn't know that all along they planned to slaughter us like animals. When the police attacked, some of us fled to Tenerías. There were hundreds of policemen crawling all over the place. A police squad followed us and shot Claudio just as we penetrated the most isolated corner of Tenerías. We hid him in an abandoned mill while the rest of us took turns guarding outside. He was badly wounded, but we couldn't move from our hiding place because there was a curfew, but one of our members was able to bring a sympathetic doctor. The doctor bandaged Claudio's wounds and gave him an injection. Before he left, he looked at me and shook his head.

"The next morning when I woke up, I found Claudio curled in a ball, his face and hands blue-black, in a puddle of blood. I couldn't straighten him out on the floor. He was my *compadre,* my childhood friend, I couldn't bear to see him like that. I massaged his legs, his arms, his chest, but it was too late."

Luis turned away from them, picked up a pinecone and turned it over in his hand.

"You lost your wife and I lost my husband. What more do they want?" Elpidia asked sadly.

✦ ✦ ✦

When they returned to Camuy, Elpidia discovered that Claudio's death had not been sufficient penalty for them. Additional payment was due. Additional payment would always be due. Two men from the National Guard stomped into the house late one night, barking orders.

"This house belongs to a traitor. You must leave immediately or we'll arrest you," one of the guards said crisply. "Remember, you can't take anything with you," he ordered as he left.

The only place they could go was back to San Juan, where Socorro's sister lived. They had stayed there during those awful days when they had waited for news about Claudio. They had no money for another journey. They sold a few things and paid off a member of the National Guard to turn a blind eye for a couple of weeks. They fished for crabs late at night and cleaned and fattened them up in cages by feeding them corn, cooked rice and bread soaked in milk. Once the crabs were fat and clean, Socorro and Elpidia boiled them in a big black pot over the wood stove. The women set up a table outdoors to pick out the delicate white meat. They rolled empty bottles over the spindly legs to squeeze out every bit of meat. Crabmeat was a delicacy and sold well in the *quintas* belonging to rich landowners.

Socorro, the family herbalist, collected the hot peppers, oregano, onions and garlic she had planted in her vegetable garden and mixed them with olive oil and vinegar to make her famous *pique,* a hot sauce relished by the neighbors to liven up the taste of beans, stews and soups.

Just before their journey, they baked loaves of bread after Socorro and Elpidia had put their gold earrings and wedding bands into the dough. They hired a car to get to San Juan. For safety, Laura's family joined other fleeing relatives of Nationalists, all women, children and old men. The younger men were either dead, hiding, in exile or in prison. The Nationalists left their homes with all they could carry in cars and small trucks. As they drove away from the only home she had ever known, Laura looked back at her house for the last time. She pressed her lips together and knuckled her eyes to hide the tears.

They stopped at Vega Baja to rest and to get food at a kiosk on the side of the road. Antonio, the driver, was not a Nationalist and could go anywhere without being arrested. He hurried back from the kiosk with the news that the island was swarming with police and the National Guard.

"We can't stay on the main road to San Juan," he said.

"What are we going to do?" Elpidia put little Pedro to her shoulder and patted his back gently.

"We have to stay in Vega Baja or Vega Alta at least for tonight, until it's safe to move on. Then we have to keep to the smaller roads. The main road is too dangerous right now," Antonio replied.

"But we don't have any more money to pay you, Antonio," Socorro said.

"Don't worry about it. One day you'll make me your great *salmorejo de jueyes,* creole crab, and I'll be happy."

"Thank you, son. God will repay you for this kindness," Socorro said.

"So, let's hit the road." Antonio got behind the wheel and turned on the ignition. Before nosing the car out to the road, he turned toward the backseat where Elpidia held the baby while Socorro changed his diaper.

"I don't know if your husband was right or wrong in his beliefs. But he was a good, peaceful man. It was a sin to kill him like that. They shot him in the back. And Ana, your *comadre* too. I'm very sorry."

"Yes, it was a crime to butcher all those people." Elpidia responded.

"You know," Socorro said, "that our neighbor's daughter got shot, and now she's paralyzed from the waist down. She's only fifteen."

"We're lucky that *la nena* wasn't hurt." Socorro bent over to the front seat where Laura was sitting and patted her on the head. "It was a miracle."

Laura listened quietly and stared out the window. She would never forget the Palm Sunday that changed their lives irreversibly. She couldn't explain it in words, but in her notebook, she drew a map of the Ponce streets where she encountered the worst terror of her life. Laura picked at the lint on her skirt and she picked and she picked, but could never remove it all.

VI

Laura had not cried in ages. By now, she thought, her eyes should be as shrunken as the rest of her body. She did not want to remember. She wanted to rinse her past away, cleanse her life of all memories. She did not have much else to do but remember and she grew weary of it. Late at night, alone in her bed, she had sharp visions of the carnage at the Ponce plaza. Faces ripped apart by bullets, broken bodies strewn on the ground, torsos hanging from balcony railings riddled with red holes, seeping like colanders. She could hear screams shattering the stillness of the night. She could feel the crush of sweaty bodies against her and the pungent odor of fear. It was all so clearly drawn in her mind. On those nights, Laura crossed her hands over her mouth, afraid of her own voice. Then the screams would crash against the back of her eyes, and she knew that they were lodged in her brain forever. She would never escape the stiff peaks of those screams. Nor could she escape the vision of Ana, like an angel floating in the room, a deep red stream flowing from her chest.

Laura lived alone now. Well, not entirely. She lived with the cat. He showed up one day out of nowhere, meowing his demands in the hallway when Laura went down to check the mail. She checked the mailbox daily, it was something to do, though no one wrote to her. On the first of the month, there were bills and her pension check. A neighbor ran errands for her and stopped by to chat once in a while. Her neighbor's world was so different, so clear with purpose, untarnished by separations and the deadweight of unrealized expectations. May God protect her always, Laura prayed.

Now, where was that stupid cat? Sometimes he disappeared for days and she was worried sick, thinking a car ran over him. But he always showed up in the end, filthy and famished, and Laura could count on his being around for a while at least.

There was nothing worth seeing on television. Maybe if she hummed to herself, the memories would drown somewhere deep inside. Maybe not. The worst part of getting old is losing one's illusions. Laura had believed for a long time that she would one day forget enough so she could hope. That time never came.

Puerta de Tierra would always hold bitter memories. It was at the pier that she and Elpidia waited for her father, who never returned. After hearing of his death in Tenerías, there was nothing to wait for. The family moved on and on, again and again, from San Juan to Río Piedras to New York, where a distant relative lived. They traveled by foot, in trucks, in ships. Elpidia wore widow's weeds to the end of her long life. She worked hard for her mother and her children. She lost everything during the insurrections except what was left of her family. They were all she had and she struggled to keep them together. The children felt secure in her love, in her devotion to them, and they knew that as long as she lived, they would never want. When Elpidia died many years later, they were living in New York City. Laura worked as a seamstress on Sixth Avenue and Pedro was away in Sacramento, studying to be an engineer. Laura was the only one by her deathbed.

When Elpidia died, Laura lost her anchor. She was driven out of New York by want, by the need to find something to hold on to, even if it was only the past cleaved into the language of her childhood. And she returned to Puerto Rico. But still she could not let go of her loss; it defined her. Her loss and she were one. She hurt for the childhood that was taken from her on a remote Palm Sunday. She was a mass of hurt, a gaping, stench-filled wound, as though she too had been wounded in Tenerías and her wound had never healed.

After the Ponce massacre, they waited and waited for justice to be done, but nothing happened. Laura had always believed that some acts could not be hidden forever, that crimes could not go unpunished. But the years had proven her wrong on that score.

For years she prayed. *God, I don't know who you are or what you are or even if you are, but I am here and I think I know who I am and what I am. Maybe it is through you that I know. But I need to know more of you. Give me a sign even if it's just in a dream. I'm so lost. Is it because I don't really know you? Or is it you who don't know me? How would I know? Except that when I hear the organ music at church every Sunday, you seem to be there.* But only there. For years, Laura prayed and prayed.

She never married. What little the family earned was reserved for her brother's education. Laura was a girl, Elpidia said. She did not need to be educated. Eventually she would marry and have someone to support her. The years dripped on like water falling on a stone. A few brave young men made tentative approaches, but Laura wanted no part of them. When Elpidia died, her last words were, "Take care of your brother." Her mother did not realize that Pedro was a man and did not need anyone to take care of him. What would become of her?

Laura still stayed awake whole nights worrying about Pedro, even after he graduated and gave her the money to return to Puerto Rico. He bought her the apartment in Old San Juan. He had a good position and was thrifty. Then he married a nice young woman from California. He had two sons, grown-up now and on their own. When Pedro visited, they never talked about the past. If Laura brought it up, he changed the subject. He was a respected member of his profession now, and she supposed he wanted to enjoy his success without thinking about the pain and poverty of the past. He had been too young to remember what had brought about the circumstances of his life. But Laura knew that he remembered all the different places they had lived in, all the changes, the poverty, all the losses. And Laura knew that if Pedro died before she did, that would be the end of her life too, because there would be no one else to remember it.

It was a miracle they were alive. In their past together, Laura and Pedro would wonder every night before they went to sleep whether it would be their last night. Every morning when they woke up, they would thank God for letting them live another day. Now, because Laura was so old, she also wondered every night whether she would live another day. But she no longer thanked God for letting her live. What was there to thank?

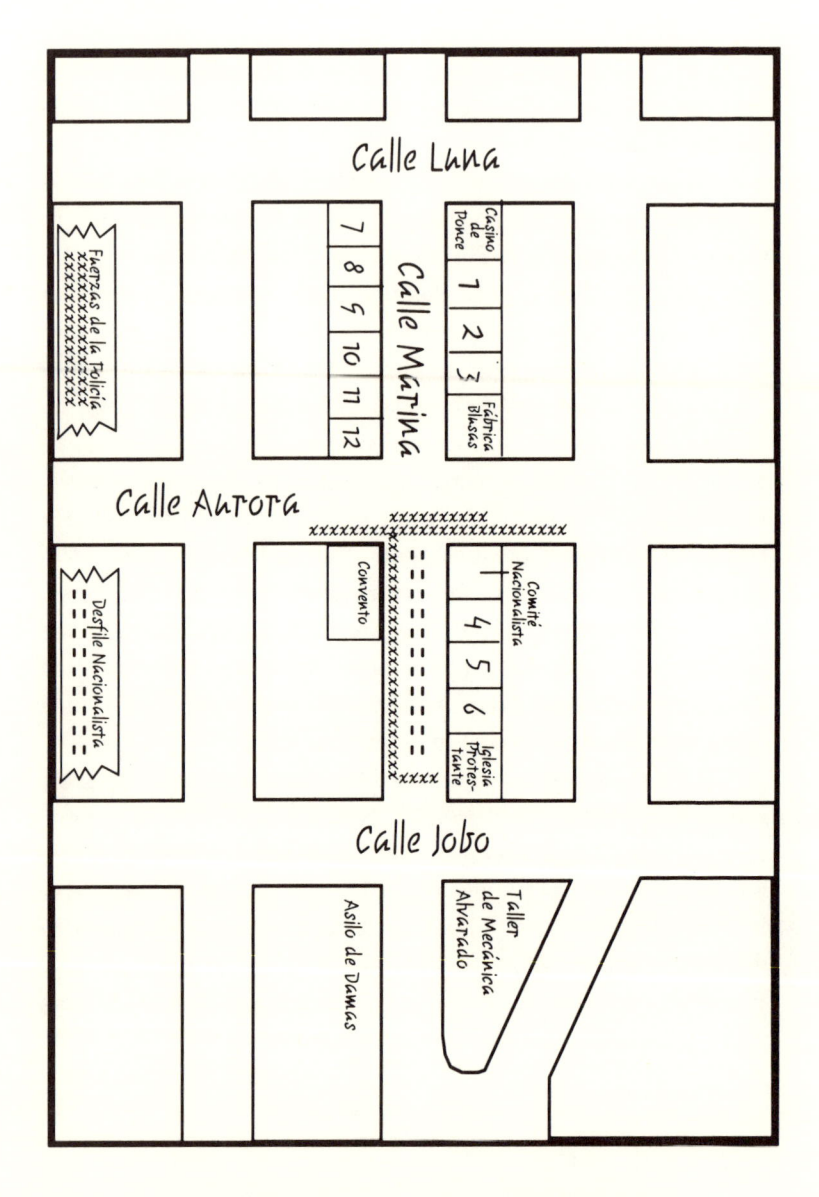

Laura's Drawing of the Ponce Massacre Site
on Palm Sunday, March 21, 1937

Letters To Mrs. Woods

Brighton High School, Boston, Massachusetts, 1980

Sara Martínez, a seventeen-year-old senior, sat in front of a large desk, speaking earnestly to the guidance counselor. Mrs. Woods, reading glasses perched at the tip of her nose, riffled papers and wrote into files as she listened to Sara. The tiny office was crammed with filing cabinets, papers and bookshelves jammed with university catalogs.

The bell rang and Sara interrupted what she was saying until the din of students changing classes quieted down in the hallway. When the period change was over, Mrs. Woods glanced at her watch and spoke to the girl with a note of exasperation in her voice.

"I really don't think you should bother taking the SATs, Sara." Mrs. Woods looked up from the papers she was scrutinizing and shook her head.

Sara sat at the edge of her chair and said nothing.

"I'm afraid you're not college material," the woman said firmly.

"But I have good grades and I want to go to college. It's important to me," Sara said forcefully.

"It's a waste of time. Don't you understand?"

"No, I don't. Why can't you give me the chance to try at least?"

"Listen, instead of wasting both our time on the SATs, I can get you into a vocational training program. You're good with numbers. How about bookkeeping?"

⁂

Boston, 1980

Dear Mrs. Woods,

You'll be pleased to know that I went ahead and took the SATs and applied to several colleges and universities.

I'm enclosing a copy of my letter of acceptance to Wesleyan University with a full scholarship. I intend to major in Philosophy of Science.

    Sincerely,
    Sara Martínez

⁂

Middletown, 1984

Dear Mrs. Woods,
    Enclosed is A copy of my diploma from Wesleyan. As you can see, I graduated summa cum laude. I majored in Philosophy with a minor in French. Thought you'd be interested.
        Sincerely,
        Sara Martínez

❖ ❖ ❖

Oxford, 1984

Dear Mrs.Woods,
I'm currently a Rhodes Scholar at Oxford doing research on the philosophy of Henri Bergson for a year. Some of the dons still remember the days when Bill Bradley was here.
    Trying to decide whether to obtain a doctorate in philosophy or study law. Rest assured that I will keep you informed.
        Sincerely,
        Sara Martínez

❖ ❖ ❖

Cambridge, 1985

Dear Mrs.Woods,
Just a note to let you know that I successfully completed my research at Oxford. I can't tell you how rewarding the experience was, both intellectually and culturally. England is lovely and I have made lasting connections with people from all over the world.

I also wanted to enclose a copy of my letter of acceptance to Harvard Law School, where I have been offered a full scholarship.

I'm sure you'll be pleased, albeit surprised.
    Sincerely,
    Sara Martínez

❖ ❖ ❖

Cambridge, 1988

Dear Mrs. Woods,
Harvard Law School was hard work, but fascinating. I was on the Law Review for a year and have been offered a clerkship at the Massachusetts Superior Court.

Here are copies of my J.D. diploma from Harvard and certificate of acceptance to the Bar of the State of Massachusetts.
    Sincerely,
    Sara Martínez, J.D.

❖ ❖ ❖

Boston, 1993

Dear Mrs. Woods,
It has been a few years since you last heard from me. I've been busy experimenting with different aspects of the law until I finally decided the judicial area that would bring me the most satisfaction and intellectual stimulation.

I thought you'd be interested in seeing the enclosed newspaper clippings regarding my swearing-in ceremony as Federal Judge for the District Court in Boston.
      Sincerely,
      Sara Martínez

Boston, 1995

Dear Miss Woods,
I have had a unique relationship with your mother since I was a senior in high school.

After all these years, I regret her passing away. Please accept my sincere condolences.
      Yours truly,
      The Honorable Sara Martínez
      U.S. District Judge

The Old Language

I

Víctor Fernández rarely engaged in anything as poetic as fury. Feasting on a cornucopia of research and teaching, presentations and writing, his life was as smooth and predictable as the annual cycles. He knew, ten years from this day, where he would be and what he would be doing. Undisturbed by past events, his days shot forward like bullets and he rarely looked back. His calendar was full of slashes and scribbles reminding him of seminars, conferences, speeches, article deadlines. He never glanced over his shoulder at the days gone by.

He had some good friends, the company of his guitar, and an occasional love affair. When he debated a professional rival at a public forum, he fielded questions with aplomb. He remained cool as marble, even when an attack became personal. He always kept his cool. That's what he thought. So this sudden anger pushing up his throat was as strange to him as wearing someone else's well-worn shoes. He swallowed deep and hard, but he could feel the stone rising again, pressing hungrily against his chest. He hated the feeling, the grotesque incongruity of rage in his neat white shirt. He was a small-boned, slim man, and he preferred to battle with concepts than with feelings. Although sometimes he did feel sad, or lonely, he was not quite sure which it was on nights when both tangled like lovers' legs and he found it hard to make a distinction.

He could feel the lonely sadness when he ate alone in restaurants. He always brought a paperback to keep him busy while he sat through the long minutes it took the waiter to bounce over with a Hi, I'm Josh. How are you this evening? Once he placed his order, he would hide behind his book so as not to face the eyes that strayed toward him from other tables. He would paste a serious look on his sadness and pretend, with a slight air of contempt, that nothing could please him more than to sit alone at a restaurant and read a good book. Though he was usually a slow eater, on these occasions he rushed through his meals and pedaled home on his bicycle built for two. Gliding through the evening haze of Cambridge streets, he resembled an extinct mammal trailing a long tail. His colleagues joked about his bicycle, but he shrugged it off. He had gotten it at a garage sale for a very good price and he was rather fond of it.

Back in his small apartment, with its familiar aromas of books and papers and the dust that collects at dusk in corners, he would sit at his computer and write scholarly articles or play computer chess and shove the sadness away. The next morning, he would wake up looking forward to his day at the computer lab or in classes, too preoccupied with his latest research inquiry to linger on sadness.

No, he wasn't prepared for the anger when he arrived on the island. Perhaps it was the sneer of barbed wires, the automated detachment of armed soldiers or maybe the scent of violence that lingered in the heavy humid air. The metallic scent was so thick, he felt an urge deep in his groin to hit, to pound, to lash out at someone in self-defense. But he buried the urge in a fold of his mind and climbed into the dark car as was requested of him.

    A deep blue strip seeped through the chain-link fences. Beyond the huge compound the turquoise ocean was calm and a lazy breeze ruffled the noon heat. In the military base black mazes scowled on the pine-green buildings and vehicles. Army jets pounced on a slick black tarmac as the automobile rose on a promontory and sliced down the avenue called La Norte, toward the military headquarters nestled in a nook of El Morro Cape. He pulled his sunglasses out of a shirt pocket, then pushed them back in. He enjoyed the vivid color and light, despite the glare bouncing from the bottle-brown hood. Tangles of palm trees surrounded the stark barracks and hangars, almost hidden by vines and hibiscus bushes. Tamarinds, almonds, and flamboyants leaned heavily against the fat clouds. Faceless soldiers sprouted everywhere, their mirrored sunglasses shimmering in the hot sun. He stared at the crew-cut head of his driver. A neck thicker than a man's thigh crouched like a ham on the uniformed shoulders. He was only a kid, eighteen, not more than nineteen maybe. Why were these children playing war games? Was the destiny of the world in the hands of these kids?

    The car stopped at a stone-gray building of ruthless geometry. Inside, his luggage was x-rayed for the third time that day and his body meticulously searched. A horse-sized German shepherd sniffed his belongings enthusiastically. The hairs on the nape of his neck prickled when the cold snout brushed his hand. Stiffly he slapped his papers on the desk.

    "Everything's in order, sir. Thank you, sir." The young stone-hewn soldier stood and saluted.

    He followed one of the ubiquitous soldiers, who seemed no different from the one at the front desk, down a barrel-view corridor and entered an air-conditioned reception room. A clone of the soldier at the front desk asked him to wait. He felt the tiny beads of perspiration on his upper lip chill and grow heavy.

"Dr. Víctor Fernández, if I'm not mistaken." A tall, uniformed man strode toward him.

Víctor smiled blankly and wondered whether it was possible to be human in a uniform. "Yes, sir, ah, Major Connors." In his distraction, Víctor almost forgot the man's name.

The major thrust his hand out. His handshake was firm and cool. He wore a white uniform with yellow-striped epaulets that looked like flattened bees. Rows of insignias, medals and tiny ribbons Víctor could not identify were pinned neatly to his white shirt. A tall muscular man, the Major led the way, like a massive iceberg, into his office.

"Sorry to keep you waiting. Have a seat." He signaled with an open hand to a chair facing his desk.

Víctor glanced at the autographed portrait of President White on the wall behind the desk and sat down. Except for a few plaques, nothing else hung on the walls. The heavy chill of the air conditioner clung to Víctor's skin, and his muscles tensed uncomfortably. It was a large, sunny room, but the dark gray walls muted the bright light streaming through the window. Major Connors strode to the large windowpanes, squinting at the light. He pulled at the venetian-blind cords and the sudden clatter drowned the hum of the air conditioner. He adjusted the slats and sat down behind the large mahogany desk, polished to a sheen, with neatly arranged piles of papers. His eyes roamed easily over the stacks. He folded his thick arms on the desk and bent his rigidly cropped head forward. The bars of light and shade from the window slashed his angular face in fragments. His face looked like a torn portrait, glued together, yet not quite whole.

"You're about ready to start your work tomorrow, I understand," the major smiled, his voice low and hard. Below the hemmed edges of the major's short sleeves, Víctor could see the tufts of blond hair on the knotted muscles of his arms.

"Yes, sir, I'm looking forward to it."

The major examined his fingertips and waited while Víctor cleared his throat several times.

"Well, I don't quite understand what it is that you'll be doing," the major continued. "Your research proposal's a bit, let's say, obscure?" He curled his mouth in a lopsided smile. His eyes narrowed and studied Víctor closely. "I'm a military man, West Point, you know, and all I know is American. Never learned another language. I figured, why waste my time? Everyone can speak my tongue, even the British." The major pulled back his lips when he laughed, baring large square teeth. "Anyhow, you'll have to brief me on this project of yours." Major Connors pressed his sun-washed eyebrows together. A severe crease cut between them.

"As indicated in my dossier, I'm a linguist at MIT." Víctor pushed his glasses up with his middle finger and readjusted the round muscles of his face. When he felt his professional qualifications were in question, he tended to bunch up and frown slightly to counteract his small frame and the narrowness of his chest.

"I thought MIT was a place for computer jocks and engineers, that sort of thing." The major stared at Víctor, narrowing his blue eyes to slits.

"Primarily, but the Linguistics Department is quite strong. Not many people know about it, though. In fact, we're still housed in military barracks similar to these. The Linguistics Department inherited the building when the ROTC pulled out during the student disturbances of the 1960s or early 1970s, at least seventy years ago. The ROTC's back now, of course, has been for decades, and they have a new building abutting ours."

"That'll keep you patriotic."

Víctor stirred uncomfortably. He wasn't sure whether the major was serious or making a humorous remark. "As you can also see in my dossier," he added quickly, "my specific professional interest is in dying languages."

Major Connors looked at him quizzically. "The old language spoken by some of the natives here isn't a dying language." He unfolded his arms, spreading the palms upward. "Why, it's spoken in many countries, as you know."

"That's true, but it's a dying language for this particular population, and I'm interested in the process by which a language dies in people's minds."

"Oh, you won't find many natives stubborn enough to cling to the old language. There're maybe a couple a hundred left. All of 'em old."

"Two hundred thirty-five, I was told by the Conflict Resolution Department."

"Well, we have orders from Washington to give you access to the natives. It's about all we can do to assist you."

Major Connors stood. Hastily, Víctor gathered his papers and stuffed them into his briefcase while the major waited, arms hanging stiffly at his sides. They walked to the door.

"By the way, you Hispanic-American or something?"

"My grandparents were from Puerto Rico. They emigrated to Connecticut sixty years ago. My parents were born in Hartford and so was I."

"I see. You understand we must be kept informed of your activities at all times, don't you?"

"Yes, I have all instructions in writing."

"Well, good luck, Dr. Fernández. Give my regards to Major Thomas when you check in with him."

II

From the helicopter, Víctor surveyed the mountain chain that cut through the island's center.

An island born of water and shaped by the trade winds, Puerto Rico is a sleepy rectangle perched on the crest of a giant submarine mountain. Its northern coast juts into the Atlantic Ocean, and the Caribbean Sea washes onto the southern littoral. The island's lush countryside teems with coconut groves, great clumps of creeper-hung trees, and inland mangroves, pressed against spidery aerial roots that help support them in the mucky soil. Dense thickets of shrubs and roots sprout among rocks and boulders. The mountain range that Víctor was now crossing rises on the island's spine, spanning it from east to west. The high green and copper flanks slope onto the fertile valley floors and coastal plains. Rivers meander through the alluvial plains at the skirt of the mountain and form deep valleys, so low that marshes, moors, and lakes cut into the soil. The greens are deep and bright, the air still and silent, the sky clear as glass. Any violence seems incongruous in the Edenic landscape.

There are times when the trade winds die in midsummer and the days of the doldrums begin. Then the northeast and southeast trades huddle close to the equator and squalls and calms and hurried airs brew, and the sky rumbles and sinks into the silent air, drowning the greens and hurling rains and winds. That's when the floods come. At other times the earth rumbles warnings beneath the surface of the sea, gathering anger like a god in the wet depths, releasing tremors, uncoiling its rocky tentacles on the land, vibrating and slashing wounds in the earth.

Now it was the helicopters, tankers and fighter jets that disturbed the island's peaceful beauty. Under the foliage, a convoy of windshield reflections flashed like knives and the popping sound of rifles was heard. Víctor wondered, recalling all the armed youngsters, whether a war had been declared and he hadn't heard.

Powdered with gray dust, Víctor looked back at the jeep bouncing away until it lurched and disappeared behind a grama-clothed knoll. He brushed his trousers with his fingertips and gathered his things. Shielding his eyes from the sharp sun with his hand, he surveyed the hamlet ahead. When he had reported to Major Thomas at the base, he said he would select his research subjects randomly. He knew the old language; he did not require a guide to get around the tiny settlement. He would have refused the ride from the base, but Major Thomas insisted it was a regulation. There seemed to be a regulation for everything.

When Víctor set out to the clutch of shacks on the hill, he realized how differently he had imagined the island. He felt like a traveler in a foreign country who had accidentally bumped into a clandestine transaction carried out by men shrouded in black in a language he could not understand. A stillness in the briny air crawled to his skull with each breath. He felt hemmed in and had the unpleasant sensation that someone was watching him. He shook the thought away.

He stopped at a graveled path leading up to the hamlet. He put down his briefcase and wiped his face with a handkerchief he pulled out of a trouser pocket. He glanced around for a place to sit and rest and finally settled on a tree stump. The side of the hill was bare, the surface scarred with furrows of darkened soil. Some patches had been razed. With the tip of his shoe, he scuffed an area where the dry earth was white as bones. A swirl of dust rose, then settled again. He waited, poised at the edge of something he could not recognize. He could feel a headache hover indecisively. He rubbed his temples, got up and walked on.

The hamlet was as bare as its soil. Rincón. So it was: a wedge sliced in the westernmost tip of the island, just above the Mona Passage. A crooked row of washed-out clapboard shacks with corrugated tin roofs teetered precariously on a hill overlooking the Caribbean Sea. Most trees had been chopped down or were yellow-leafed and dying. Underneath, where the sand stretched to the eroded hill stones, a barbed wire fence surrounded the hamlet. A tall steel chain gate, locked in rust and sunken in the sand like a drunkard, held the residents at bay. Huge reflector lights surveyed the territory at night. Víctor looked around him and was surprised to see no soldiers in the hamlet. He approached a tiny plaza which glittered like a star. An old man sat on a bench under a lone palmetto. He fanned himself with a square cardboard stapled to a flat stick. When he saw Víctor, he sighed and stiffly got up. Víctor showed him an address. He had cashed in on many favors for it. The old man pointed his gnarled finger at a shack poised at the outer edge of the settlement.

Víctor lingered in front of the shack and wiped his face again. It seemed like the place described by the old man. The shutters were unfastened and the door open. Curled in sleep, a mottled dog lay in the shade under the tiny porch. Chickens scratched the dry caked earth. The scrawny dog stirred and barked dutifully when Víctor approached the steps. He rapped on the doorjamb. "Hello," he called into the darkness.

From the shadows, he heard a creak. A dark figure stepped tentatively forward, a hand over her eyes in anticipation of the brightness outside. She was an old woman, slight and bronzed by the sun.

"Good morning," the old woman said, but looked at Víctor suspiciously. "What can I do for you?" she asked in the soft, rolling, vowel-filled tongue, using the polite form which is inevitable when speaking to strangers in the old language.

"My name is Víctor Fernández, *señora*. I've just arrived from Massachusetts and I'm looking for my great-aunt, Doña Luisa Sánchez. I was told at the plaza that I could find her here."

"I am indeed Luisa Sánchez, young man, but how do I know you are who you say you are?" She squinted at the slender figure cut boldly against the midday light.

Vistor smiled. "Here, you can see for yourself." He pulled a package from his briefcase. The old woman stared at the age-splotched manila envelope. She stepped out into the sun to examine the sepia family photographs. Her creviced cheeks hung heavily.

"Oh, my dearest sister, my beautiful niece. I can now see the resemblance. You have my mother's bold eyes, we all do. How old were you in this photograph?"

"Twelve."

"You haven't changed much, except you're thinner now. I heard about your mother's death some years ago through a smuggled letter. I suppose we're the only ones left in the family. A young man and an old woman." She shook her head. "Somehow it isn't right. Unless you have children?" she asked hopefully.

"No, not yet. I would like to talk to you, if I may." Víctor glanced inside.

"If what you want is to talk, someone up there must be answering my prayers." She pointed toward the sky. "But what am I doing? Where are my manners? Come in, come in out of that harsh sun. Please pardon the modesty of my humble house. Would you like some coffee?"

"No, thank you," Víctor said, knowing it was not polite to accept right away.

"But I was just ready to prepare some for myself. Please join me."

"All right, then."

Luisa still brewed coffee with a colander, the old way. She used the thick cone-shaped cotton sock gathered at the top in a circular wire that extended out into a long handle. The conical sock was wide on top and narrowed to a tip. She worked quickly on a double range tabletop kerosene stove. She stirred the dark aromatic coffee grains in boiling water until a thick brown foam floated to the surface. Then she poured the mixture through the cloth sock into a clay pitcher. The smell was sweet and strong, like honey. The color was burnt gold. She boiled milk, as was the custom, and with a small wire strainer sifted it to remove the thick-seamed skin that collected on the surface. She talked incessantly as she worked.

"The man you met at the plaza, Julián, he's my only friend, a kind of guardian angel. He's always at the plaza, sitting like a ghost in judgment. Every few days he drops by at sunset and brings me milk, bottled water, things like that. I don't need too much to eat. I give him some eggs and a bunch of the green bananas I get from the plants growing in the empty lot at the back of the house."

She eased herself carefully into a hemp hammock threaded at the ends with thick ropes and tied around stakes in the bare unpainted walls. She blew delicately into her coffee before drinking. Víctor sat in a Spanish cedar rocker, one of the few pieces of furniture in the shack. Lazily, he sipped the sweet strong brew. The rocker creaked. He remembered languid summer afternoon naps in his grandmother's bed awakened by the sweet aroma of her coffee.

He glanced around the one-room shack. Behind the hammock was a narrow bed, neatly covered with a blue chenille bedspread. Next to the bed, a small wooden crate served as a nightstand. On it was a dusty shadeless lamp and a few books. A poster, puckered and water-stained, hung over the headboard, the only bright spot in the shack. Víctor got up to examine it closely. It was Miguel Pou's *Los coches de la Plaza de Ponce,* representing a Puerto Rican scene that existed over a century earlier, more like what Víctor had expected to see on the island. But the date under the artist's signature was 1926. A long time ago: a time of horse-drawn carriages and massive trees with exuberant clusters of feathery flowers and those long evening walks around the plaza, called *la vuelta.* The stories his grandmother had told him gathered like misty veils in his memory. A memory of a place he had never seen, yet through his grandmother's words, he remembered well.

"One of the few things I've been able to keep," Luisa said. "The poster and the rocking chair. Even the bed's not mine. Borrowed it from the base people. I'm living in a stranger's land. There is nothing I recognize anymore. The island has changed so much. I always think of the big breakthrough in bamboo research." She looked at Víctor solemnly. "When the bamboo dies, the panda dies. But that is neither here nor there, is it?"

She smoothed her skirt. "I was so surprised to see you. I never thought someone would remember. But why did you come, Víctor? This isn't a vacation paradise anymore. It was once, you know, long before you were born. Tourists flocked from all over the world, especially North Americans. The island was beautiful then," she said longingly.

"I'm here to study the old language spoken by the native population. I'm working on a book," Víctor responded.

"A book, that's good, very good," she smiled and nodded. "Are you a linguist or a journalist?"

"A linguist."

"Ah, a scientist. That's even better. Too many foreign linguists have come here to study us, like guinea pigs. Anthropologists and sociologists too. They don't even speak our language. They studied the twentieth-century literature of Spain, of all places, and think they can understand us. Our literature, with a magic of its own, is of no interest to them.

Since they cannot understand what we say and what we write, they claim we're linguistically deficient. Never occurred to them that the deficiencies were theirs. They never made any attempt to study our own language, literature and values. Why, that awful book Oscar Lewis published about us was a disgrace! He saw a lot, but understood nothing. So all we got from him were misinterpretations. Then, that arrogant British man, I forgot his name, a so-called historian, he enjoyed our hospitality during several months, and then wrote a terrible book that revealed only his ignorance of our history. Yet it's what those people wrote that was published by prestigious university presses, not what our own historians had written. It would take years to tell you about all the shoddy scholarship we've been subjected to and the many times we've been portrayed so wrongly to the world. Since *West Side Story,* it's been downhill all the way.

"Oh, well," she sighed deeply. "I can't count on many more years to see any changes. I live from day to day. I'm just glad to have seen the day when the work is done by someone like you, a native speaker, someone with a heart for it, not just sterile scientific curiosity full of silly preconceptions. Your parents were smart to teach you the old language and our ways."

"Yes, I was lucky."

Víctor spoke about his upbringing, the work he was engaged in at the moment, and weather conditions in New England. When he felt the necessary time for polite conversation had elapsed before engaging in any serious discussion, as was the custom, he asked, "Tell me, *tía,* how is it that so few people speak the old language now in Puerto Rico?"

"Puerto Rico, you say it so beautifully. It slides and forms little tides and quakes on the tongue, doesn't it? Ah, the pleasure it gives me as it rolls from the lips down to the soft palate and throat. They pronounce it Poe-roe-ree-coe now." She shuddered.

Víctor pulled a small black recorder from his briefcase. "Do you mind?" he asked.

Luisa went to the door, plucking at the skirt that clung to the back of her thighs. She stretched her neck out and scanned the surroundings carefully. "Never know who's listening," she muttered solemnly before easing into the sagging bottom of the hammock once more.

"Go ahead, go ahead, there is no one around."

She waved a hand at him and waited, hands folded on her lap, while Víctor tested the first few seconds of the blank tape. "You want to know how all this came about? How many years do you have?" Her gleaming dentures clicked when she laughed. When he was ready, she asked, "Have you read any of the books and articles?"

"Yes, I have, but no one seems to tell the true story, the complete story. There are too many inaccuracies and too many gaps left unaccounted for in the literature."

"I know," she said. "There has been much written in English. A lot of silly nonsense and hypocritical humbug as I told you before. Whatever was published here, in our own language, was never disseminated."

She sat up straight-backed, smoothed her skirt and cleared her throat. Gently, she eased into the past. Her words cracked the turquoise afternoon.

"Puerto Rico was an island in the sun. It had everything: fertile soil, eternal summers, fruits dripping from trees, and vegetables springing from the earth. Even the heat was never unbearable because the trade winds blew softly over us like a soothing whisper. I was born in 1946, that was 94 years ago." Her voice lingered over the memories. "I was an occasional translator and a full-time history teacher, so I know a little about language."

She paused for a long time. Víctor sat quietly, waiting.

"Then our world came crashing into a void. I remember it all too well. I was fifty-two years old when our woes began in earnest. I spoke English as any educated Puerto Rican did, but after the ordeals, English died in my mind and my heart. I have spoken only our old language since then and can communicate only with my generation. The young, those who stayed with their families and were allowed to attend the military schools, learned only English. Soldiers thronged through the island and strung barbed wires and built barracks. Many of us were relocated to this tiny hamlet in Rincón. I lived in Río Piedras then, on the other side of the island, where the University of Puerto Rico used to be. They call it Stone River now," she added mournfully.

"I was in school, teaching, the day it happened. The morning was sunny and almost cloudless. Nothing unusual had happened that day, except a student in math class had an epilepsy attack. I heard the commotion because my class was next door. The girl was screaming and writhing on the floor. Then we heard the tanks and helicopters. Someone turned on the radio and the governor was exhorting the population not to worry, it was just a maneuver. Some maneuver. About fifty soldiers burst into the school with machine guns. We could hardly hear the soldiers' orders, the children were screaming and crying so much. They herded teachers and students into a truck and we were all forced to march single-file, hands at the back of our heads, into a huge room with long wooden benches out in Fort Buchanan. There we were stripped, examined and questioned. The children were taken to a separate room and teachers, the principal and secretaries were called one by one to a small office. We were terribly nervous and didn't know quite how to react to it all. I remember it well, I certainly do.

"'Sit down,' a young soldier ordered. 'Do you speak English?'

"'Yes,' I answered as I watched him write on a sheet of paper neatly placed in a gray folder.

"'What's your name, ma'am?' I straightened my back and answered, giving him my two surnames, as we were accustomed to in those days. I had to spell them for him.

"'What's your profession?' he snapped.

"'I am a history teacher at Juan Antonio Corretjer High School.' I had to spell that too.

"'You teach in the native language don't you, 'cause your English's not so good,' he said.

"I was insulted. I have a Ph.D. in Modern European History from the University of Chicago. My English was excellent. Then I realized it was my accent—he was fooled by my accent.

"'Yes, I teach in the native language,' I responded.

"'Well, you're no good in our schools,' he declared and he slapped my folder shut. 'Wait outside, ma'am,' was the last thing he said to me.

"I waited for six excruciating hours. I could hear the children weeping in the next room. My head swam with confusion. The Comparative Literature teacher sat next to me. Hands to her head, she swayed back and forth, mumbling something I couldn't understand. Another soldier gave us some weak coffee. I can still remember my numb buttocks and the cramps in my toes. And the children's sobs. Declared unfit to teach in English by the young soldier, I never worked again." Luisa's milky eyes rested at a point far back in the curve of time and she sat very still.

Víctor examined the dark rim in the bottom of his cup. He walked out to the tiny porch. The sky was still blue and the sun sharp. He frowned and peered out at the calm sea before going back in.

"Will you be staying at the military quarters? You can stay with me, if they allow it, you know. I might be able to get a cot for you at the base," Luisa said.

"They don't allow it. It's one of their regulations." Eyes downcast, he added, "I'm only authorized to have contact with the 'natives,' as they call you, for the purposes of my research. No socialization is permitted. In fact, I'm not allowed to meet with more than two native people at a time when I'm recording. Those are their rules. I'm sorry, *tía*."

III

The next morning, Víctor arrived at Luisa's shack early. He placed his tape recorder and briefcase on a small rickety table that slanted sideways with the weight. A row of pens lined the pocket of his short-sleeved cotton shirt. He hurried out again and walked around the shack to make sure no one was around. In the shack he fiddled with the recorder. Luisa turned on an oscillating fan that whirred loudly and muffled their voices. While she prepared coffee, she leaned over the sink, thrust her head out the window and peered earnestly around, eyes squinting in the sun. When she was satisfied that no one was listening, she sat next to her nephew. Knowing that Víctor was allowed only a few days to collect his language samples, she pressed ahead.

"During my lifetime, I've seen many things," she said. "I saw the Cuban Revolution and the flocks of Cuban refugees that flooded our shores. The Duvalier era and all the Haitians escaping to our island. Not to mention waves of Dominicans, Colombians, Argentinians. Everyone fleeing the turmoil at home and seeking haven in an American territory where they could speak Spanish.

"I saw American liberalism die and so-called 'Rambo Reaganism' emerge. I have seen death so many times, my eyes are swollen with blood. So many Puerto Ricans have died in the wars, in secret scientific experiments for the pharmaceuticals and the military, in the famines. Our population grew. But our fertile soil became fallow and the factories idle. The infamous status question sucked in generations of our people and paralyzed us. It was resolved at the beginning of the century, 2001, to be exact, when the President of the United States and Congress declared Puerto Rico a military base. Interesting how it occurred right before our very eyes."

"What happened?" Víctor tilted forward.

Luisa took a sip of water and swallowed hard. She placed a hand over her mouth, afraid of her own words. She went to the door. "We don't have much time left. Can you stay a bit longer today?"

Víctor glanced at his watch. "We have a little over an hour."

"Yes," Luisa said. "That's about right." She sat in her hammock.

"What happened, you ask? It's a story straight out of a political conspiracy novel. Unbelievable, that's what it is. In those days, you see, the statehooders were the most conservative element in Puerto Rican society. The pro-statehood party was called the New Progressive Party, which was just a new name for the old Republican Party here. It was composed of right-wing Puerto Ricans and many foreigners, who dreamed of living in a real state of the United States. Ever fearful of the autonomist movement in the Popular Democratic Party, the party in power, the statehooders, decided to take covert action in collusion with Washington. At that time, the Republican president of the United States, who used to be head of the CIA—imagine that—startled us by declaring a commitment to statehood for Puerto Rico. We all shook our heads. What are they up to in Washington, we wondered. Puerto Ricans who lived in the United States had traditionally voted for the Democrats, you see. And if Puerto Rico became a state, island Puerto Ricans would probably vote for the Democrats too. It just did not make any sense. Well, with full support from the President himself, the statehooders infiltrated the Popular Democratic Party and won seats in the island's Senate and House of Representatives by expounding the familiar autonomist rhetoric.

"They were wolves in sheep's clothing and no one suspected their true identity. Finally, one of the imposters was elected governor, and that was the end of it. Still under the autonomist guise, the statehooders rigged a referendum on the status issue and declared that the Puerto Rican people had chosen statehood. At this point, their mask was slipping, but they controlled the police force and, of course, the FBI was actively assisting them. They also had the full cooperation of all those federal government agents in Puerto Rico who said they worked for the Department of State, of all things. So they eliminated all opposition.

"Complacently, the statehooders offered Puerto Rico to Washington on a silver platter. The Puerto Rican people have voted for statehood, they declared. Yes, yes, Washington said. Golly that's a real good thing, the president said. Ah, but they had read the North Americans all wrong. You see, the United States was not interested in granting us equal status. It was not our rights they were concerned about. At the time they were involved in covert military activities in Central and South America. They called it the "war on drugs." That was their code. What they really wanted was a strategically located military base for their incursions in the whole Caribbean basin and Latin America. Not to mention the able-bodied Puerto Rican men and women who could fight whenever it was time for an invasion. There had been several invasions by then.

"So by fiat, instead of a state, the island was declared the biggest U.S. military base in the world. A provision was passed in Congress that the Puerto Ricans who wanted to stay could. There were few jobs, though, because all the technical workers were brought in from the United States. Most Puerto Ricans left. There were some rebellions by young men and women, but the FBI promptly brought trumped up charges against them, and they were either accused of conspiracy to overthrow the government of the United States, or diagnosed as mentally deranged. After the trials, all held in Boston, by the way, they were sent to federal prisons or state-run asylums for life. That was the end of that."

"Why isn't any of this documented in historical research?" Víctor asked. "I've read everything I could get my hands on before coming, and historians agree that Puerto Ricans decided, in a referendum, that the island become a military base."

"It's adulterated history, *sobrino*. The chroniclers of our times have distorted events to conform to the image the United States wanted to present to the world. And frankly, no one cares. There were no journalists here seeking the truth. No human rights organizations. No one. Who are Puerto Ricans in the eyes of the world, after all? We are the invisible people."

Víctor glanced nervously at his watch and rubbed his temples. "It's time, *tía*, the jeep will be picking me up any minute."

He moved quickly, soundless as a cat. He wrapped the tape in the rags Luisa handed him and nestled the package in an old cookie tin. He then lodged it under a floorboard. Grimacing with the effort of keeping the noise down, he moved the stove table over the floorboard. Then he slipped into the recorder a tape of previously recorded conversation about everyday events, like the afternoon rain squall or the merits of Seville oranges. As he snapped the catches of his briefcase, they heard the jeep pull up. Luisa sank into the dark folds of her hammock when Víctor hurried down the steps.

IV

Víctor held on to the overhead rail. The jeep stumbled down the unpaved road, jostling and bouncing. Luisa's coffee sloshed in his stomach. It was just like those horrid roller coaster rides he pretended to enjoy in his childhood. Once down the hill, the driver leaned heavily to the side, pulling the steering wheel down. The jeep swerved sharply onto a wide paved road leading toward the base. Soldiers lined the parallel edges of the road, standing boldly under the shady trees, semi automatic weapons resting in the crooks of their arms.

When Víctor jumped down from the jeep at the Officers' Club, he realized he was gray with dust. But he didn't have time to change. The driver escorted Víctor directly to the dining room. Víctor could hear the soft tinkle of knives and forks on the china and the murmur of conversation. Lunch was always called for, what was it, thirteen hundred. He glanced at his watch. It was one-thirty already.

"Enjoy your lunch, sir," the young driver said. Víctor was as flustered as usual when the young man saluted him. He was at a loss for words, wishing he could shake his hand or poke him in the shoulder, or something other than watching the soldier lift the wooden arm of a mannequin. Víctor stared at a rectangular pin the young man wore. His eyeglasses were so dusty, he could not see the name clearly.

"Oh, yes, thank you, you too, 'bye," he managed to muster.

He brushed his trousers with the palm of his hand and polished his eyeglasses before walking in.

It was not his favorite time of day. He wished he could avoid eating, so as not to be subjected to this daily torture. But he had to check in at midday anyhow. Besides, he was hypoglycemic and could not withstand a whole day without food. Already his cluster migraines were frequent enough without adding more stress to his system. And he was terrified of going to the base doctor, a tall, white-haired man with sinister eyes. Víctor remembered reading an old book his father kept about the CIA mind-bending experiments on unsuspecting subjects that occurred during the mid-twentieth century, just before and during the Vietnam War, and he shivered. There was no way he was going to risk becoming a guinea pig. No way.

Still shaking his head, he hurried into the large dining room. The waiter was a native, a young man who had never acquired the old language, as Víctor learned when he attempted to recruit him for his research project. The waiter stared at him blankly for a few seconds and then led him to a long table where several officers were seated. Major Thomas, the commanding officer, stood up and shook his hand.

"Well, what do you know, our friend the linguist is here." The major acted as though he had not seen Víctor in years.

Several pairs of pale blue eyes looked at him blankly. Heads nodded.

"Have you all met?" he asked the walls.

"I think so," Víctor responded quickly and fell into a chair.

As soon as he smoothed a white linen napkin on his lap, the waiter placed a bowl of soup in front of him and filled his water glass.

"How 'bout a beer?" the major asked.

"No thank you, I have work to do this afternoon."

"Oh, come on, is that all you do around here?" he laughed. "There's lots of good golf and marlin fishing in these parts."

"My stay here is brief, and I have a lot of work to do."

Víctor cast a sidelong glance at the major, who had quieted down substantially while he carved his steak with great precision. Víctor took a sip of the soup. Cream of broccoli, one of his favorites, but much too salty. They must make it with bouillon cubes, he thought, and pushed his plate away.

V

Darkness settled exuberantly in the evenings. A deep rose, tinged with lavender and tiger-lily gold, collected gently on the slate clouds, and then faded into the night. Víctor liked to watch the sunset from his window and listen to the tiny Puerto Rican frogs called *coquís*. The tiny frogs existed nowhere else in the world. He wondered whether this was a sign of hope.

He had one more day with Luisa and then he had to move on. But move on to what? To Julián, the old man who sat at the tiny glimmering plaza all day and drowned his thoughts like unwanted kittens? To the grandmother who had lost her sons in the wars and her grandchildren to a language she would never speak? The full moon was mellow with its own weight. Its beams of light spilled into Víctor's room. He plugged his earphones in and switched on the tape recorder.

When he returned to Cambridge, he would analyze the data collected. His research proposal had promised to develop a taxonomy of the old language. Based on that, he would write his book and scholarly papers. But his original intentions were lost in the night, when he tossed in his bed and stooped figures gathered in the shadows of his room and gave him no rest. Luisa's words haunted him like old scars. He felt inexplicably ashamed, though he was not responsible for the rude transformation her life had experienced, nor was he responsible for the events that caused the death of a language in the minds of a people. Then he realized he was ashamed of his blindness. Yes, he was also guilty of averting his eyes as the rest of the world had done. He paced restlessly, no longer caring about semantic nuances or shades of pronunciation in the old language. For Luisa's words were truth. Syntax and morphology and pragmatics and communicative competence and turn allocation and allomorphs, the core of his very life, rapidly eroded in significance before the force of her words. Those words were naked and brave. Exposed, they trembled in him. He was almost relieved to feel a need awaken, a yearning he had held at bay. For, at just that moment when an atavistic anger shook in his heart and curled his fists, he recognized the stone in his throat.

VI

Julián waited at the foot of the stairs. Ancient as the wind and bent with the weight of too many memories, he turned his good ear to Víctor's voice. That first day at the plaza when Víctor spoke to him in the old language, Julián seemed to recognize him from somewhere. At first he thought he was dreaming, given as he was to succumbing to catnaps during his long days on the hard plaza bench. He had been mute to the outsiders for a long time. He had listened to the foreign garble that jarred him until mercifully he stopped hearing it and was struck with the mute stubbornness of weeds. When he saw Víctor, that first time, he knew. Despite the foreign habits and clothes, Víctor had the scent of the soil in his blood, and it clung to his skin like sweat. He could not hide his roots. For many years Julián had visions in his sleep of a knot of sad-faced men, surrounded by words, and Víctor was one of them. Julián recognized Víctor's true identity even before the young bespectacled man had spoken to him that day. Now Víctor was in the shack sipping Luisa's aromatic coffee.

"You are us," Julián said to him from the door and turned his head east, his nostrils flaring in the sea-scented air.

"We waited for you, you know. At times it seemed we would all die and with us all things would extinguish, for our voices have been silenced and our books burned in the darkness. But you have come like a miracle to avenge us with words. We are glad the enemy has not recognized you. They are blinded by their own intentions. They hope to use what you discover to learn more about us and keep us more firmly in their fist. But when you swooped down into our hamlet, we took in the scent. Then we heard you speak the old tongue and we knew it was you we had been waiting for."

"I don't understand. What's this all about, *tía?*" Víctor turned to Luisa, who had gone out to guard the porch. Hastily, she came back inside.

"We don't have much time, *sobrino,* so today we'll reveal that which has been silenced for fifty years."

She walked out again, looked around and, satisfied that no one was listening, she returned whispering urgently to Julián. Luisa and Julián huddled over a dark package at the foot of the bed. Víctor joined them when Luisa beckoned silently with her hand.

"We will not be overheard here. We checked the area for surveillance equipment. None was found," Julián said mysteriously.

Julián rose slowly, his flat face a mass of grooves. He heaved a large burlap bag on the bed. Reverentially, he pulled books from the sack. One by one he placed them on the bed, the yellow light that slanted through the window spilled on the titles. Gently he patted the last one, though it was not dusty, before putting it down. He glanced out the window, alert, but all he saw was the clear sky. The strong sea breeze brought nothing but salt to his old nostrils.

Víctor's heart lurched. He was almost sick with excitement as he read the titles in the old language. He had read some of them, the ones he had inherited from his parents and kept in a glass-enclosed bookcase in his Cambridge apartment. Some titles he had only heard in his grandmother's voice: *Usmail, La ceiba en el tiesto, Caballo de palo*. A distant rumor slipped into his memories. Then the old man spoke.

"Only eleven of the classics survive. The pyre and censorship destroyed the thousands of volumes of poetry and fiction and essays written by our authors in the old language. A holocaust of words. We have memorized some and the cherished words have kept our memories ablaze, for they exist only in our minds now. But we must make these known.

"Many researchers have come to our shores. They have attempted to cajole us, bribe us, threaten us to give up our memories. But we have resisted, for only one of ours will treat our legacy with the respect it deserves. You will take these books with you and the world will finally know the awful silence we have been condemned to live."

"You're giving these to me?" Víctor asked in disbelief.

"Yes, you will take the books that have survived and today we will start reciting the ones conserved in our memories, for it is late and we are very old. But beware, do not let the enemy know what it is that you are doing with your recorder."

"The military doesn't seem too interested in what I do," Víctor replied.

"Besides, they already know I'm recording the old language."

"One never knows what they are up to," the old man said. "When they stifled our voices, the world never knew what really happened. They believe we are now harmless because we are so old and do not speak the universal language. They believe no one is interested in what happened on this tiny island so many years ago. They can pretend to be liberal by allowing you to come in and study our ways. What they do not know is that you can rewrite history, a history that will not be flattering to the enemy. Do not reveal a thing until the time is right. If they were to find you involved in this venture, you will be destroyed. Have no doubt. We do not want any more bloodshed. Enough is enough."

Víctor switched on the tape recorder and listened to the spangled flow of words that spilled and rolled and thrust from the old lips cracked by the silence of time. Words as beautiful as love and relentless as passion. The words folded under his skin in silky cocoons and sang and wept and throbbed until they soared again into the air. The voices quivered with the beauty of the words. When they were finished, Julián and Luisa wept, pressing against each other. Their tears were the tears of grief for what was lost.

Then they heard the unmistakable scuff of boots. Víctor stood up, clutching a book to his chest. Julián restrained Víctor by putting a hand on his shoulder and shaking his head sorrowfully. The boots advanced. Quick, hard, closer and closer, like the terrible rumble of the earth before it quakes. The boots halted in a long stretch of silence snapped by the repeated kick of rifles. Luisa sat very still, humming an old forgotten *danza*.

The Curse

When the sun climbed over the shantytown in Santurce, Puerto Rico, it lingered just above the milk-white moon for a moment's lull before spilling an amber haze over the jerrybuilt shacks. The light formed a silky web on the juts of tin roofs, the planes of cardboard and the grid of dirt roads, so the shantytown seemed enclosed in a dome of veiled glass. This impression lasted for a few minutes only, for as soon as the sun gathered strength and its heat intensified, the shantytown revealed its true stark ugliness.

The stench of the canals, pungent as rotten meat, had not yet risen with the heat when Celeste stepped out of her shack and crossed the creaking board that spanned the mud channel. The poorest of the shantytown dwellers built their tar paper and cardboard shacks out in the muddy marsh that collected sewage from Miramar mansions. High stilts propped up the shacks and wooden boards stuck out like tongues over the mud. The boards were slung to dirt roads that wound toward Cervecería Corona, the brewery, and to the narrow paved streets ending in Avenida Fernández Juncos.

Celeste, whose skin was already the color of polished copper, unfurled her blue umbrella as a shield against the hot sun. She rubbed her protruding belly and just as she was about to set out among the shacks that crowded the warren of dirt roads, she saw him. A tall slender man sat on a pockmarked log near the huts across the dirt road. He was watching or waiting, she could not tell. Celeste had seen him many times before. When she asked about him in the neighborhood, no one seemed to know who he was. He always seemed to hide his face by turning around or pretending to wipe himself with a handkerchief. She looked at him warily and hurried away, a tingling sensation crawling up her spine. Overcome by a coughing fit, Celeste dropped the umbrella and held her bulging stomach. She turned to the mud channel and spat out the sticky phlegm. She picked up her umbrella and shook off the dust. When she looked back, the man was gone.

Celeste was only seventeen, yet she felt so tired she could sit right there on the dirt that was crawling with red ants. But she had to keep going, quickly, or she'd be late for work. A sun-darkened woman, hip encumbered by a bucket of water, was coming from the communal faucet that was down the street.

"Still going to work, Celeste? Aren't you about due now?"

"Doña Esperanza says in a few weeks."

"Heard anything from Roberto?" the woman asked slyly.

Celeste stiffened. "Why do you ask?"

"Oh, nothing. This bucket's heavy. *Hasta luego.*"

Celeste stared angrily at the woman's stiff back as she walked away without another word. Roberto was never coming back. Everyone knew it. Even Celeste. She had tried everything to make him return. She hollowed a gourd and filled it with thyme honey and the purest olive oil she could afford. She wrote Roberto's name on a bit of paper and dunked it in the gourd. She then floated a wick on the oil and lit a flame for five days and, dressed in yellow, prayed fervently to Oshún. The great god refused to listen to her pleas. That was when she lost all hope that Roberto would ever come back to her.

✦ ✦ ✦

Rows of one-and two-story wooden structures lined the Avenida Fernández Juncos. They were built mostly with *ausubo,* called ironwood because it was so resistant to termites and the rot caused by mildew. Some of the buildings were shops and others were residences for local merchants. Thinking about Roberto, about his empty promises and betrayals, Celeste crossed the busy avenue. She was startled by a farmer's cart that rumbled in front of her loaded with fresh mangos, avocados, and green bananas en route to the marketplace in the center of Santurce. One of its wheels squeaked piercingly and sparks of dust lodged on her skirt and sandals.

She rushed to the other side and stopped to catch her breath. She gazed past the shops and the noisy people cramming the avenue, past the peaks of coconut palms and the cloud banks on high, to the shimmering mountain with ridges thrusting against the blue sky. She had been born on that mountain, but when she turned fifteen, her family had been driven by desperation to move to the shantytown in the capital city, where they hoped to find work after there was no work to be found on the plantations. Her father died shortly after moving to Santurce and her mother followed him soon afterwards. Her only brother had drifted to New York before Roberto had disappeared. She had not heard from her brother in over a year. Roberto had been gone for months.

The church bell announcing the morning Mass at Sagrado Corazón reminded Celeste that she had to move quickly if she was to stop by the store before going to her seamstress job at the linen-shirt factory. She hastened past the bread women gliding along the blue mist of the morning with golden loaves on their heads. Oblivious to the fishmongers hawking the day's catch, dogs barking at carts, shopkeepers flinging their shutters open, Celeste reached her favorite shop. Don Sebastián, the shop owner, was engaged in serious haggling with a crusty old man. The object of negotiation was a black umbrella. The storekeeper tenderly stroked its thick panels.

"It's a prince of an umbrella," he said. "And because you're a regular customer, I'll give it to you for three pesos. A bargain."

The old man tilted his head back and snorted disdainfully. "What are you talking about?" he appeared shocked. "This isn't worth cattle dung. Look at it. It's faded by the sun."

"You're crazy. This is a work of art. But for you, I'll make a sacrifice. You can have it for two pesos, and that's as far as I can go," Don Sebastián said haughtily.

"I'll give you one," the patron offered with a tone of disgust. "Take the peso now, before that wreck of an umbrella crumbles in your hands. Besides, who wants an umbrella anyway? It hasn't rained in months. It'll probably never rain again."

"What? You don't know what you're talking about. This fine umbrella will make an excellent shade for the sun. One peso..." Don Sebastián smirked. "That won't even pay for the handle."

The haggling seemed to go on forever, so Celeste squeezed into the tiny shop, incongruously called *La Grande,* and headed toward the counter. The shop was stuffed with jugs of candy and golden treacle, barrels of raw sugar and rice sacks, so closely packed that if one item were to be removed, everything would tumble to the ground. There were sewing notions, brooms, fly swatters, and knickknacks no one seemed tempted to buy, for they were almost black with dust, hanging precariously on rusted hooks from the walls.

When Celeste looked around, she saw the umbrella patron wrinkling his face and walking out of the shop with all the scorn he could muster in his expression. Don Sebastián rested against the doorway, sucking deeply on a fat cigar, appearing indifferent to it all.

Celeste closed her eyes and almost swooned. The smell of heady moisture trapped between the rafters and under the shelves mingled with the sharp odor of mildew and had saturated the stuffy shop. When her dizzy spell passed, she stared longingly at the huge candy jars on the counter, then she heard the umbrella patron talking to Don Sebastián. He had come back and fixed a determined gaze on the umbrella once more. Don Sebastián pushed the umbrella into the man's hands.

"So you're back. Listen, this umbrella is fit for the King of Spain. You can have it for one seventy-five," he said.

"One fifty."

Don Sebastián beamed. The patron crooked the umbrella handle on his forearm and, with a satisfied look, handed the shopkeeper the coins.

"Good afternoon, Don Sebastián," Celeste greeted the shopkeeper when the patron left. "Business any better?"

Don Sebastián squinted through the gray smoke of his cigar and shook his head. "See what I have to go through to sell a miserable umbrella? It's as hard as swimming upstream, but one has to live." He slipped behind the counter and uncovered a candy jug. "The usual?" he asked.

Celeste nodded as she eyed the candy avidly. *La Grande* was Celeste's favorite shop, for in this small mine she could find the best coconut sticks in San Juan. It was worth the detour, she thought.

Once outside, she opened the brown paper wrapper and selected the tallest, thickest coconut stick. She unfurled its paraffin paper, folded it carefully and put it in her purse. She inspected the sparkling white candy, twirling the wooden stick between her fingers, as its sweet aroma filled her nostrils with pleasure. She would eat this one quickly because it was the first. As the brown wrapper became leaner, she would pace her portions more slowly, so that she would not be deprived of her luxury for too long before she got paid and could renew her supply. She was salivating when she slid the candy very slowly into her mouth. Unable to contain herself any longer, she sucked on it greedily. She tasted the chunks of coconut that clung suspended in the sugary mass and bit into it. But when she swallowed, a thick wave of nausea rose unexpectedly from her stomach. She broke into a cold sweat and her hands and face became clammy. She ran to the curb and vomited violently.

✤ ✤ ✤

Still wiping her face with a handkerchief, Celeste arrived at the shirt factory. She and her friend Mariana joined the cluster of seamstresses at the stairwell. The women took their positions at the ground-floor sewing area while the men climbed to the second-floor cutting room. As soon as Celeste heard the factory whistle, she hung her head over the sewing machine and clamped the presser foot down. As she raised an arm to spin the wheel, she felt faint and pressed her forehead against the machine.

Mariana looked over her shoulder to make sure the supervisor was not around and came up to her friend.

"What's the matter, Celeste?"

"I'll be all right. You better get back to work before they catch you." Celeste wiped the thick beads of sweat from her forehead and forced herself to get through the morning. At noon, when the whistle bleated again, Celeste and Mariana took their brown paper bags and went out to a cobblestoned patch behind the factory that was shielded by a sheet of corrugated zinc. Celeste had difficulty rushing through the pack of workers, and the spot was crowded when she got there. But Mariana had held a place for her by anchoring her hands on her hips, elbows far apart, making herself as ample as possible. The women groaned while massaging their aching backs and stretched toward the puff of breeze that came through. Mariana munched on water bread and some cheese she had unwrapped from a bit of banana leaf. She unscrewed a thermos and poured some steaming coffee with milk into the lid.

"You're not eating?" she asked Celeste.

"Can't swallow a thing." She pulled out her precious bag of coconut sticks. "Not even these."

"You have to eat, especially in your condition. You were ready to faint in there."

"It's like a fist twisting in my stomach, and my chest hurts so much I can hardly swallow."

"You should go to the hospital."

"What's a doctor going to do? It's a curse. I know it. Someone put the evil eye on me, and I'm going downhill. Everyday I get worse. Have to see the *santera,* that's all."

"Know a good one?"

"The one in my barrio is good, all right." Celeste nodded vigorously. "A few months ago, I had a really bad headache caused by a curse. I told you before how that Delia has it in for me. Well, Doña Jacinta poured coconut milk over my head and then made a paste with coconut meat and cocoa butter and rubbed it on my scalp. She prayed and prayed in Yoruba with lots of lighted candles on her altar and by the time she was done, my headache was gone."

"Think Delia's at it again?"

"No, Delia doesn't have that kind of power. It's someone else, I'm sure of it," Celeste answered.

Darkness was swooping down when Celeste finished her work shift and made her way as quickly as she could manage to the shantytown. The sun had not set, but a full moon bloomed at the back, smudged with shadows at the edges. The pale blue sky was streaked with tints of pink and lavender.

Once at the shantytown, the sharp odor of pig swill, goat hide and sewage that rose from the mud turned her stomach even as Celeste held a handkerchief to her nose. Her large belly propelled her forward, deeper into the labyrinth of dirt paths and shacks.

"Doña Jacinta," she called into a shack of faded boards. An old, stout woman, the color of ebony, appeared at the doorway. She wore a red turban tied with a knot in front and a white smock. Five bead necklaces were draped over her breasts. She was smoking a fat cigar. When Doña Jacinta embraced Celeste and kissed her left cheek in the traditional *santero* greeting, Celeste was comforted by the pleasant scent of sandalwood mixed with tobacco that surfaced on her skin.

"I have to talk to you, Doña Jacinta."

When the older woman saw Celeste's pale face, she gripped the young woman's elbow and led her inside.

"Would you like some coffee?" Jacinta asked.

"No, nothing, thank you, Doña Jacinta." Celeste sat down when the *santera* motioned toward a rocking chair. "I came to see you because, um, because..." Celeste mumbled nervously, eyes darting around the sparsely furnished shack.

"Speak up, *m'ija*, you're having troubles. It's clear as a cloudless sky. I can feel the troubles in your presence."

"I'm feeling worse every day," Celeste said, voice thick with tears.

"It's another curse, you know. This is a difficult one," Doña Jacinta added, eyes darkened with concern. "We'll have to work harder and more carefully because of your condition." She sat back and puffed at her cigar thoughtfully.

"I managed to save enough money for the *derecho*."

"Just put the coins for the *orishas* in the pot. The saints will be pleased with whatever your offering can get for them."

Celeste placed the coins in a clay jug on the altar Doña Jacinta had fashioned from pinewood in the darkest corner of the shack. The altar was covered with a fishnet, white jasmines floating in a jar of water and a large shiny stone, almost perfectly round, with cowrie shells for eyes and mouth. Surrounding the stone were wood carvings of the Virgin Mary and Santa Barbara, several lit candles, a coconut, copper pennies, a small bottle of sugarcane syrup and a pint of rum.

"That's good," Doña Jacinta nodded when Celeste paid the saints' *derecho* and reached for the sugarcane syrup. She anointed Celeste's temples, lips, wrists and ankles with the syrup. Then she took the coconut, broke it open with a small hammer, and poured the milk carefully into a clay pot. She placed seven copper pennies around the stone head and sprinkled it three times with water while mumbling prayers Celeste could not understand. Then she inhaled deeply from her cigar and blew a dense cloud of smoke on Celeste's face.

"Take this coconut milk home and pour it over your head," Doña Jacinta said after she made the sign of the cross.

"Make sure you do this at your doorstep just before you go in. And come back to see me tomorrow. You've got a strong spirit mounted on you. It's going to be difficult, but I'll prepare the things we need for our work."

※ ※ ※

Celeste knelt clumsily beside her cot. If they would help her get rid of this curse, she prayed fervently to the Virgin of Guadalupe and Saint Jude Thadeus, she would offer them novenas, rosaries. Then she reconsidered and, since she was desperate, she offered to wear a habit in the saints' colors for a year. She crossed herself and struggled to get up. Her swollen legs were numb and she crumpled to the floor. She waited until she felt the blood circulating once more. Once in her cot, she turned the knob of her kerosene lamp and lay in the pitch-black darkness, listening to the breeze settling down in the marsh. Thoughts of Roberto crowded in her mind again. He had left her to fend for herself and their child, knowing she had no parents, no relatives in the city. Whenever she realized her predicament, Celeste was gripped with fear and a sense of desolation. What in the world would she do once the baby was born? And she felt so awful all the time. Every night her legs were stiff with pain from sitting at the sewing machine all day. And the blood she spat out every time she coughed. And the constant retching. She had to get rid of this curse. But first she had to find out who had cast the spell on her.

When Isabel fell asleep, she plunged into a nightmare. The shack was tightly sealed and she clawed at the walls until blood gushed from her fingertips. Then she looked over her shoulder and behind her, swaying in the breeze, was a dress hanging limply from the ceiling. It was her mother's dress, and she knew her dead mother's spirit was there in the shack, invisible, unapproachable. She struggled to wake herself, she tried to scream, but she lay petrified, breathing hard but not making a sound.

When the dawn light crept into the shack, Celeste opened her eyes and rubbed them with the heel of her hand. She was dead tired. Sleep had brought her no rest. She padded to a tin basin, poured some rainwater into it and splashed it on her face. She dressed and rushed out to the factory, already dreading her evening session with the *santera*.

✦ ✦ ✦

"Good evening, Doña Jacinta."

"Come in, I'm alone." Doña Jacinta pulled up a chair for Celeste. "I've been working for you, but the work's been hard, very hard," she said wearily. She sat on a small wicker chair next to Celeste. Her face was drenched with perspiration. She fanned herself with a piece of cardboard.

"There's a bad influence on you, and it's bad, very bad."

Jacinta sat quietly, eyes closed, hands folded on her lap.

"Ohhh," the woman moaned suddenly, clenching her eyes. She flung her head backwards and plunged into a trance.

"Oh, good spirits, come to me now when I need you. Take away this flood of evil descending on me. Oh, take it away, I can't bear it. Ohhh, ohhh."

Jacinta moaned and shook her head violently from side to side in a syncopated beat. Then she stood up, perfectly erect like a wooden statue, her eyes deep and round as puddles. She put a clammy hand around Celeste's wrist and led her to the altar. She had spread a white cotton mantle over the fishnet and lit several blue candles around her *orishas*, virgins and saints. Jacinta sat opposite Celeste and, with splayed fingers, palms down, drew circles over a jar of holy water she had pilfered from church one Sunday when no one was looking. She circled the water, tracing an orb with each hand as if she were waxing a glossy table. She muttered prayers under her breath, her dark eyelids clamped over visions of evil that struggled to gush forward like an ocean wave. She invoked the spirits, black and white, young and old. The spirit of Obatalá, old as the world, Changó, who embraced Santa Bárbara, the white virgin of the Spaniards, and Yemayá, the Virgin Mary, the kind mother of the *orishas*. Pagan and Christian, she pronounced all their names in a long incantation that spanned several continents. Jacinta moaned her low hoarse song. Her head lolled to the sides, eyes tightly stitched. With fists at her sides, her elbows battered against her sides like a hen flapping her wings. Tremors shook her core like a roaring whip. Her chair fell back and she writhed on the bare floor.

Then a voice sprang from her throat, the scratchy voice of a man at the edge of the world. The hairs on the nape of Celeste's neck stood on end when the voice cackled loudly, maliciously, and Jacinta shook and trembled like a mass of congealed fat.

The voice seemed to emerge from a place deep in the earth's core. Its message rose not from the woman's mouth, but from a long narrow tunnel somewhere under Celeste's feet. It rose swirling like smoke, lapping Celeste's hem. She recoiled in horror. She wanted to shut her eyelids, sew them together like seams, stuff her ears with mud and arrest the stench of oil and brine and sulphur clogging her nostrils. She reared up like a cobra when the voice uttered the unutterable.

"I'm taking your soul, Celeste. I'll gather you like a bunch of roses and present you as a gift to the Evil One. Then you'll be mine until time is endless. You don't recognize me now, do you my sweet and tender girl? I'm no longer tall and lean and handsome. Just a voice clutching at you from the entrails of the earth. But I had a name once. Before you were born, I had a name. I don't exist now because my name rests on no one's memory. But I will tell you, my sweet, sweet girl. My name is Octavio. Do you remember now, my Celeste, how you detested me because I was older and wanted you so badly? You were a little girl then, but I wanted you. I would watch you through the oceans of cane as you ran to the river. I watched you every day from sunrise to sunset. Then, remember when I tried to have my way with you, make you mine completely, how you struggled, my sweet? You screamed and bit me and then your father came and swung his machete into my throat. But I haven't forgotten you. I was ready to wait, bide my time and yours, until you were ripe and ready to come to me. Ah, but you were very willing to surrender your charms to another. I won't have that, my sweet. Your love for Roberto, my enemy, is cursed, Celeste, because I have cursed him, and you, and your love. I died for you, and that means you are indebted to me forever. You are mine. You will always be mine, for all eternity. Celeste, my Celeste, my sweet. I'll never relinquish my hold on you."

Celeste fell in a feverish tangle. She swayed and veered away from the rattling table while the *santera* moaned on the floor. She rushed to the steps and breathed in the evening air, her chest was burning. She had held her breath so long, her lungs hurt. She attempted to lower herself gently down the steps, but her knees shook violently, unable to sustain her. Celeste slid down the wall and eased herself onto the top step until the tremor subsided.

✦ ✦ ✦

When Jacinta emerged from her trance, she pronounced solemnly, "It's very bad, my child." She dabbed her forehead with a handkerchief. "The spirit is as evil as they come."

Celeste looked out at the night and felt herself crumple, dissolve into the dark sky.

"No, Celeste, you have to be strong and brave," Jacinta shook her and gave her some smelling salts to bring her out of the fainting spell. She pushed back the hair that stuck to the perspiration on Celeste's forehead.

"I'll work with you. It won't be easy, though, but I feel stronger, stronger than the spirit. We'll work together until he's gone forever. If not, he'll never let you live in peace," she said ominously and gazed at a distant point on the horizon as if reading a hidden word. "There'll be no peace around here for a long time." She shook her head sadly.

Celeste returned to her ordeal whenever she could find bananas or ripe mangos or some pesos as offerings to the *orishas*. The two women huddled around the small table, chanting and praying. The altar was laden now with the saints, rosaries and reliquaries Jacinta usually kept burrowed in a low wooden box. The spirit would grip Jacinta and screech and writhe with her, scraping his angry fingers up Celeste's thighs. He was in agony. But Jacinta was old and tired. The opponent was young, strong and evil. He had the power to tire her, but she had the good spirits and the clarity of her will on her side. The struggle was hard. The weeks seemed to grope through time, but the evil spirit's grip on Celeste held.

One day, Jacinta said, "Go on home now and don't return. I'll come to you when I'm ready."

Celeste inhaled slightly.

"No, don't ask any questions. When the time comes, and I'm sure it will be soon, you'll know. Now, I have to deal with the spirit alone."

❖ ❖ ❖

When Celeste reached her shack that evening, her head was splitting with pain. She held her head in cupped hands, elbows resting on her rubbery knees. She rocked back and forth in silent dejection. Every now and then she emitted an involuntary moan deep from the confines of her throat and it slipped through her parched lips to punctuate the throbbing, pounding sledgehammer in her scalp. The suffocation she felt in her room was intolerable. She searched the dark shack, seeking some relief. She stumbled in the dark, bouncing weakly against the walls and door frames. Driven by an unrelenting anxiety, she flung her head over the windowsill and retched.

Many days and nights passed until Celeste was so close to birthing, she could no longer clamber up the alleys to go to work. One morning, dawn was climbing slowly and Celeste pulled back the faded cotton scrap nailed to a cleft which served as the shack entryway. She looked out at the other shacks standing precariously on stilts. When the tenuous morning light seeped into her shack, she saw the man sitting on the log across the way. He looked over his shoulder, got up quickly and tore away, brushing the seat of his trousers, just as Jacinta showed up on the road and crossed the board to Celeste's shack.

"Now, Celeste, it's time we did some work together."

"Oh, Doña Jacinta, do I have to? I'm so heavy and I've had one of those splitting headaches all night. Anyhow," she ventured hopefully, "maybe the spirit's gone by now."

"No, no, *m'ija,*" Jacinta shook her head. "It's here with you all the time. I brought it with me for a while and struggled with it very hard. I know he's a little weak now, but he's back here, with you and your child. I fear for you now, Celeste. You have to work with me or the spirit'll get strong again. Then you'll be in his absolute power, and I won't be able to help you. Nothing will save you then. Come on, Celeste, let's start our work, you don't have a choice."

Jacinta untied the string around a brown paper package she had brought. It contained several candles, a jar of holy water and some pennies. She smoothed a white handkerchief on the table, placed the jar of water on it with the lid off, and lit a candle on each side of the jar. She dipped a finger in the water and crossed herself several times, then she crossed Celeste. She dipped into the jar again and sprinkled holy water on her arms and on Celeste's forehead. She pulled Celeste down with her, and they both knelt on the floor. Jacinta beckoned her powers with her mind and Celeste remained quietly at her side.

When the sun slipped behind the cloud banks, the light in the shack thickened to a dusty bronze. Night fell quickly.

Jacinta's face gleamed in the candlelight. Celeste lay on her cot, arms resting on her chest.

Then they heard the cry of an infant. The women stared at Celeste's bulging abdomen, their eyes widened with horror.

"Oh, God help us, he's trying to get to the baby. Quick, Celeste, put your hands over the holy water and pray, pray as hard as you can."

"What do I pray?" Celeste cried desperately. Her mouth dried up and her upper lip stuck to her teeth.

"Our Father, Hail Mary, anything to keep him away. Here, take this cross and put it over your belly. Hurry, Celeste, hurry."

Jacinta squeezed the young woman's hand and they prayed hard. Jacinta panted and fell backwards. She fought the spirit, sweat streaming down her face and mingling with tears of desperation. She shook and trembled like an earthquake, her voice clogged in her throat so she could not articulate a word. The spirit mounted her, she opened her mouth and the howl of a wolf, low and piercing, squeezed from her insides. Celeste prayed hard and clamped her eyes shut.

After what seemed like a long drawn-out time without time, crawling at a pace that was not human, Jacinta got up. She said wearily, "He has to follow me now. He knows I'm his enemy and that I've come between you and his force. I have to deal with him alone," and she left.

Celeste was rooted to the floor. She knelt there for hours, praying and crying, until she collapsed in a heap in front of the altar Jacinta had arranged on her table. The candles guttered and were doused out by the wind while Celeste slept.

❖ ❖ ❖

Jacinta cut quickly through the alleys. It was a long distance to her shack, and her legs felt rubbery and weak after the day's efforts. She was following a tiny tamped path when she heard steps behind her. They were heavy, ponderous, giant steps that pounded like an echo in her brain. Dogs bayed and she heard the whir of wings. Then she felt a scalding breath on her neck and she broke into a rickety run, panting heavily, desperately gasping for breath. He was certainly strong and lithe. She was no match for him, not in the outside world, not without her weapons.

"Our Father, Olorún-Olofi, who made the world and everything in it," she muttered under her breath. "Oh, help me, St. Jude, Alabbgwanna, with this desperate cause. Babalú-Ayé, Virgen María, Santa Bárbara, Elegguá protect me from this evil spirit." She called all the saints, African gods and goddesses, Christian virgins. She called on God himself. Yet she heard the dogs baying, the heavy steps, pounding, reverberating at her heels.

She was near the swamp. It would be easier to run in that direction for there were worn paths around it. But just as she got there, the fiery breath was on her face like scalding acid. A rush of black wings thrust her into the swamp.

Celeste slept fitfully. She was awakened by heavy steps on the creaking floorboards. She was fully awake when she saw a shadow coming through her shack, approaching her slowly. She stumbled out of bed. She groped for the matchbox in the dark and lit the kerosene lamp by her cot.

Under the dim light, she recognized the shadow. It was the man who sat every morning on the log across the road. Her heart thumped like a drum when she tried to run past him.

The man held up his hand and Celeste was struck by an inability to move. She stared at him wildly. The man spoke in a voice that was deep and hollow, like wind in a tunnel.

"You still don't recognize me, my sweet?"

Rage is a Fallen Angel
For Marina Catzaras

I

He said I had to be in here for two months.
At least.
I said, no way. And he said, or the public mental hospital.
I said, where do I sign?
I'm still fuming about it, but can't let my anger show.
Dr. Rhodes thinks I'm pliable. I suppose he was trained to believe everyone is. He gives me these silly tapes about unrealistic expectations and thinks that I listen to them. He thinks a lot of things that don't really exist.

All the lies I tell him, for example. But then maybe the lies do exist, once he believes in their existence.

Does something exist when it's only in someone's mind? Are lies not lies after all as long as someone believes them? Are lies lies if you think they're true? Maybe it's a matter of intent. Are lies not lies if there is no intention to lie?

The first time I remember lying, I hadn't even lied at all.

I was a little girl visiting an aunt in Ciales. One of my cousins and I returned from an afternoon walk to the river which was just behind the house. My aunt asked me about the walk and whether I had seen any freshwater shrimp. It turns out I hadn't. So I said, "No, *tía*," shaking my head vigorously, the way little girls like to do to show off their curls. In my case, I had new earrings on.

But just as I said this, and to my astonishment, my cousin said, *"Oh, sí, Mamá,"* and embellished her tale of unseen shrimp with florid adjectives and the wildest superlatives you can imagine. She was around twelve then and dreamed of becoming an actress. She was always practicing her art, as she called it. My aunt was furious because she thought the worst sin was to lie to a relative, and to lie to her, who was almost my mother, was certainly a serious transgression. She dragged me into her bedroom and forced me to kneel before a bloody Jesus on a wooden crucifix she had on the wall and beg for God's forgiveness. It was so humiliating, especially since my cousin kept peeking into the room and snickering through my entire ordeal.

✤ ✤ ✤

Getting back to my lies to Dr. Rhodes, I suppose that the person who believes the lie is as important in this matter as the one who tells it.

What if I tell someone I went to Egypt and that person believes me? Does the lie both exist and not exist? Is it a lie in my mind, yet a reality in the other person's mind? When the person then goes on to tell someone else, you know so-and-so went to Egypt, does that constitute a truth? What if, having never been to Egypt, I become convinced that I did go? Is it true then? At least as far as I'm concerned?

Does it all boil down to teleology, then? It's not enough to describe something, nor to understand its cause and effect, we must also know its purpose. Or better said, the end that moves something. It's the only way to completely understand it. In other words, we must know why something is what it is. I know this sounds a bit Aristotelian, but I can't help having read all the books that I've read. It's the result of a liberal arts education. Sometimes it's a real burden.

I wind up entangled in an idea that spawns another idea and another and another until I can't remember where the hell I was going with it all. It's really disturbing.

But I have to write the ideas and what sparks them, so I can remember everything that I've learned. I'm not being arrogant by trotting out all the knowledge I've collected. It's just that I have to remember all that I'm forgetting. I must remember. I must.

The shocks don't help. They call it ECT. Electroconvulsive therapy. Everything's disguised in acronyms around here. Like the MMI, as though we couldn't figure out it was a test to determine whether we're paranoid or schizophrenic or both. It's all part of that secret language they have. And they assume we're too stupid to figure out their silly codes. Patients are supposed to be excluded from the professionals' clique this way. Oh well, this isn't the only place where language is used to exclude.

The rubber-sheeted bed is slick as ice. I start trembling every time they wheel the black machine to my bed side.

Which is often. Twice a day. Every day.

The big black box on a trolley. The tube of lubricating jelly. The mouth gag. It's hard not to stare at the knobs, the cords, the switches. The nurse plugs the machine in and the dials glow in the early-morning gloom. My stomach turns.

At first I begged them to give me a sedative to help me relax. They said it wasn't necessary.

This is how it goes.

Dr. Rhodes adjusts the settings on the black box and rubs jelly on my temples. He orders me to blow my nose, breathe deeply and open my mouth so he can fit the gag between my teeth. I clamp my mouth on the gag and shut my eyes. I feel something hard pressing against the sides of my head. I heard them once refer to these as electrodes. Dr. Rhodes holds the electrodes and orders the nurse to punch the button. I struggle and moan.

Go! he says and I feel a searing flash of pain. Then they do it again. And again.

And again.

I forget everything for a while. Then things come to me, things I haven't thought about in ages. This happens a lot when I can't sleep. Which is too bad because I like to sleep. That's when I feel no love or hate. But during those long stretches of insomnia, I become aware of my heart palpitations or worry about what to do with my arms and I can't sleep. Then an idea pops into my head and I keep thinking about it, worrying it in my mind, like a dog gnawing on a bone.

Like karma. I've been thinking about karma all the time. After sloshing it around in my mind for days, I realized that the concept of karma was generated by the privileged classes. To make sure the oppressed accepted their lot in life. That is, a life of exploitation by the very same privileged classes that thought up this karma business. And thus, secured their status. You can be sure it wasn't the poor working slaves who came up with it. What's in it for them, after all?

I really become agitated thinking about this. People rarely get what they deserve. Look at Hitler. All my life I had thought people were compensated for what they did. After all, I was already a teenager in the late sixties. If people were good, good would come to them. If they were cruel, vicious, mean, terrible people, they would pay for their acts. Like dying a slow agonizing death from pancreatic cancer.

Then I realized that this wasn't necessarily so, if you didn't believe in reincarnation. Which I don't.

Which made me think. I refuse to be born again. No way. I fought birth like mad the first time around (first, that is, if reincarnation doesn't exist, oh, please don't let it be). Anyhow, I was born buttocks first, cursing the world like a full-fledged Maori.

I was never meant to be, I think.

When the river spilled blood, I had been walking the path of the perfect place somewhere deep in my mother's darkness. Then I don't know what happened, but I got shoved out. And here I am, to make a long story short. Something I find congenitally incapable of doing.

"Here" is a psychiatric hospital in Hartford. Dr. Rhodes said I had to be in for two months. But I think I've been here longer than that. But I'm not sure. I forget things, so I'm really not sure about anything. Or something might be one way now, but who knows how it will be a moment from now?

I'm not insane, let me clarify that from the start. Not yet, that is. Even though I sometimes have to look at my photograph, the one I always keep in my gown pocket, to remember what I look like. They don't have mirrors here, you see.

Whether I wind up insane or not depends on how long I stay in this hospital. Mill said that good cannot engender evil and evil cannot engender good. This disputes Giordano Bruno's coincidences of contraries theory. (Lucretius's too.) Well, I might side with Mill on this one. As far as I'm concerned, this place is bad. No good can come of it. The longer I stay in here, the more likely it is I'll go mad. It's human nature. We adapt easily.

Dr. Rhodes says the shocks will help me deal with what happened to my baby. I've forgotten a lot of things, but I haven't forgotten my baby girl. When she died, suffocated in her own vomit, the world turned its back on me. I swallowed thorns that night. I became stone. I'll never forgive the world its lovelessness. Its cruelty.

In this place, I'm finally grasping the true meaning of silence. A concept that echoes in my mind like a nightmare. There's a place at my core where words don't exist. Where I discovered the multiple dimensions of pain. The core of desolation, loss and rage. It's what was left after my little girl died and my pain had no words. There's nothing worse than the inability to name your hurt. Will I ever be able to attach words to my loss?

That's when I rage. And I hate and I rave and I pound on the table and scream, no more, I won't take any more. And I cut myself with knives, and when they take away the knives, I cut myself with plastic forks, whatever there is to hurt myself more. And then they hide everything from me, but I find a plastic cup and I crush it in my hand like a freshly laid egg and there I find that in the mess, there is always an edge. That's all I need to open my flesh, to make blood flow from myself. To feel relief from the terrible rage.

❖ ❖ ❖

Like Prince Hal in *Henry IV*, I ponder on ways to cope with rebellion. But if I run away from something, do I run toward something else at the same time? What I mean is, do I continue this pretense of pliability? I said Dr. Rhodes, like all shrinks I suppose, thinks people are pliable. I wonder if he thinks the same of himself? Does a psychiatrist consider that he is an exception? Sort of how religious fundamentalists think that only they enjoy the grace of a god.

It's so difficult for me to organize my hope.

As I said, Dr. Rhodes thinks I'm pliable, but I'm really not. I need desperately to rebel. Even if it's just to kill myself. Now I rebel in little ways, of course, so they don't certify me incompetent. Unless they've already done so. I don't trust this Dr. Rhodes. That's why I lie to him all the time. If I told him the truth, God only knows what he would do with it. Turn it around to hurt me, I suppose.

That's how they all are. Men, that is. Men who happen to be shrinks, especially. Can't trust them for a second. One minute they're talking to you in a soothing, almost motherly voice, and the next they're threatening to commit you to a mental institution. Just because a person's depressed after having lost everything there was to lose. And tries to commit suicide. Having no intention of hurting anyone. But herself. So what business is it of anyone's? It's not evil or anything as long as you don't hurt someone else.

Don't get me started on that one. Because what I hate to think about most of all is the nature of evil. I can really get stuck on it, like a scratched record. And can't seem to extricate myself.

Sometimes I don't tell the truth, but it's only because I don't know what the truth is. So I make it up. And it becomes real. So real I could taste it. Somehow I feel like the Egyptian god Ptah who by the mere act of thinking and speaking brought the world into existence.

That's why I'm a writer. Or was. To create my own world. To be my own god. (Heaven forbid I ever tell Dr. Rhodes this!)

I used to be a poet, then wrote screenplays.

Sort of like Anthony Burgess, who wrote music before writing novels. In an interview he once said that for years he was trying to write an opera about Sigmund Freud, but was having trouble with the libretto. I wonder if he ever finished it?

I was writing a script about a salsa queen's rise from the slums. I wonder if I ever finished it? Often, the most difficult thing for a writer is knowing when a work ends. One could spend a lifetime on a poem or a novel or a story or a script. What with all the revisions and everything. It's a miracle we ever finish anything.

What I said before about lying regarding a trip to Egypt isn't true. Though I may have given that impression. I did go to Egypt once. I remember being struck by the Egyptian word for bread, which is the same as the word for life. Eish. Sounds like a complaint.

I had the misfortune of visiting the Temple of Kom Ombo, that double temple of the crocodile-headed god Sebek and the falcon-headed god Horus. They were both actually one god, a god who was half good and half bad (reminding me of Bruno's coincidences of contraries theory).

With my propensity to dwell on this nature of evil business, I squandered the rest of the trip wondering whether evil lurks in me too. Maybe I shouldn't have sat on the clammy sarcophagus of the mummified crocodile, even though my feet were killing me. Maybe I entered the temple on its bad side. Maybe I sniffed too deeply of the ammonium chloride that is said to have been first made in Alexandria from the dung of camels, ammonia that could have easily wafted south to Aswan.

But I had terrible nightmares after that visit. Were they nightmares or visitations from ram-headed gods intoxicated with camel dung? How would I know?

Even lolling on the east side of the Nile in a felucca each sunset offered no solace. Even the smiling Egyptians.

Actually, the smiling Egyptians had little to smile about, which really got me going on the injustices of the world. Here you have people who believe that they live under a law of universal justice, and go about smiling as though it were true. As though the voluntary maiming of infants, so they can beg in the streets, or the bombing of mosques and tourists, or the hunger and constant dust and thirst of the implacable desert didn't exist.

Tutankhamen lies dead with crook and flail on his chest, that's what I always say when I have nothing better to say.

※ ※ ※

My first husband, Pepe, was Puerto Rican like me, but looked Egyptian. He was tall and dark and smiled a lot. Except that Pepe frittered away his time on this and that. I'm not entirely sure what he did. Maybe nothing. Well, what can you expect from a man you meet on the San Juan to Cataño ferry during off-hours.

He was the only person I'd ever met who called Mohammed Ali, Cassius Clay. He liked classical music, but didn't know much about it because when he was growing up, they only had Bach in his house. Then he read somewhere that the Japanese had discovered a cure for baldness: Mozart. But not all of Mozart. Only Concerto Number 3 for flute and harp and Piano Concerto Number 21. Pepe had an intense preoccupation with his physical appearance. Counted the number of hairs on his comb every morning and worried about his hair loss for the rest of the day. We listened to a lot of flute, harp and piano for a while. His hair never grew any thicker, though.

Pepe had some annoying habits that drove me up the wall. He straightened and twisted his arm to snap the elbow joint all the time. In the middle of the night I could hear his snapping elbow and felt murderous. That wasn't his most annoying habit, though. He liked to collect and file clippings from newspapers and magazines. I couldn't invite people over for dinner, because invariably Pepe would get into a discussion with someone, and when he wanted to make a point, he'd rush to his files to search for the relevant article that would prove his argument. Sometimes, hours would go by before he returned. By that time, the guests would jump out of their chairs and rush out the door, afraid of getting into another discussion with him and having to put up with another one of his searches.

Pepe was brought up in the city, but he liked to believe he was a country boy. Once, we were invited by some of his relatives to their *finca* for a weekend. Our first morning was uneventful, except we stepped on some warm cow pies and had to rush to the river to clean up. Then on Sunday, Pepe's cousin made the mistake of saying she needed to slaughter a chicken for dinner. Pepe, in his usual self-assured manner, strutted up to her and volunteered to do the job. No sweat, he said, but not before instructing me to record it on his video camera. Sometimes he knew full well I hated to do. I have an ingrained fear of cameras. I think Balzac was right when he said that the self is peeled away like an onion every time a person is photographed.

Anyhow, I found myself under the blazing sun, holding the idiotic camcorder while Pepe shrieked directions. He grabbed a squawking guinea hen, jammed its head into his fist and wrung its neck while he yelled directorial instructions at me. "Get over here, you're too far! What're you doing? You stupid or something, can't you see the sun's behind you?"

When he flung the hen to the ground, it bounced back up, feathers ruffled, and scrambled off into the bushes. I was dutifully recording the hen's flight to freedom when Pepe snatched the camera out of my hands.

"That's enough," he growled, and stomped into the house.

I was so bored during that marriage that I read my way through all of Chekhov and discovered how ordinary heroes really are. My problem is that I expect ordinary people to act as heroes. But there are few heroes in the world, and it's hard for me to accept the ordinary, especially in myself. But even heroes have frailties, Chekhov says. Heroes are ordinary people who rise to an occasion. That sounds pretty Chekhovian to me, but I think my second husband told me that.

I loved him very much. But I can't remember what happened to him. It's all a blur. The death of my baby girl. Slicing my wrists with a kitchen knife. I really wanted to saw my hands off, but fainted when I saw all the blood.

Does death destroy love? I wonder.

Falling in love is different from loving, I've discovered.

An editor once said to me that I get lost in metaphors and literary allusions. She was right. I'm doing it right now. It's my way of hiding the pain of truth. I do it in therapy all the time. Dr. Rhodes never knows what I'm talking about. But he pretends to.

Here he comes. Dr. Rhodes, that is. His white robe flapping. Better hide the journal. Quick.

II

Last time I wrote, Dr. Rhodes had come to see me. His eyes were wide with excitement. Said I needed surgery. A hysterectomy. I stopped menstruating when they locked me up in here. Even though I'm still too young to be menopausal. I can't remember my age exactly, but the doctors have figured it out. The staff gynecologist thought I should have everything scooped out. It's a new kind of cancer prevention treatment, Dr. Rhodes said. Who did he think he was kidding? I wondered if they'd remove my testicles if I were a man. That's what's called an academic question, isn't it?

I wouldn't agree to sign the papers for the operation, and Dr. Rhodes started getting snippety with me. It's either surgery or an indefinite stay here, he said. Or the state mental institution. I said, where do I sign?

I couldn't write for a long time after the operation. I was so depressed.

The Mayans believed that when you cut down a tree, you must ask its forgiveness or else a star will fall out of the sky. I wonder what happens when a woman is eviscerated for no good reason. Will the sun fall out? Or the moon?

The walls seem to press against me. I draw the curtains, so I won't have to face the day and wonder about all the good things out there I might be missing. Complained of a migraine, so as not to arouse the suspicions of the hospital staff. They gave me a pill and left me alone.

I think about the mutilated women in Picasso's art and wonder why men need to mutilate us. Even symbolically. I wish Dr. Rhodes and the staff gynecologist had been harmless artists, instead of what they are.

The Ibans killed their enemies, then scooped out the brains through the nostrils. They tore off the cheek skin and ate it to ensure fearlessness. They decorated their sheaths and sword hilts with the shorn hair. Jaws were fastened, tongue cut off, head smoked over fire. They decorated the eye sockets with brightly colored studs and put wooden stoppers up the nostrils.

Are women the enemies of men?

Once, Dr. Rhodes accused me of having penis envy. Penis envy, my foot, I thought. Privilege envy is more like it. I didn't tell him that, of course. It would only prove his point.

✦ ✦ ✦

After shock treatment today, I felt as though I were in a big black hole full of nothing. I was so afraid the hole would suck me into its nothingness. Now, I'm afraid to live and afraid to die, all at the same time. I wish I could scream.

I have no one to talk to in here. So I have conversations in my head. I ask questions and answer them, discuss problems with myself, presenting the pros and cons to every argument. When the nurses or the other patients talk to me, I'm too tired to talk. I do talk to Dr. Rhodes, if only to lie to him. Tell him I'm fine. Today he told me I needed more of everything they're giving me. How do I get out of here. I can't seem to escape.

For days, I've heard nothing but the howling and sobs of women. They've been giving us therapeutic injections every day. The world seems different now. Noisier.

I can recall things I had forgotten. Things that happened years ago are so clear in my mind. Too clear, like a blinding sun in the white desert. I'm writing everything I can remember. So if I forget, because of the shock treatment or the injections, it will be conserved somewhere. Then I can read it and know what I have learned in life, what I've lived through. I just wish I could remember what happened to Jaime and my little girl. I wish I could remember just that.

I do remember odd things, like Pepe and his guinea hen, like that school I worked in once, after Pepe and I got divorced.

❖ ❖ ❖

I couldn't live on my poetry—it wasn't that good. And the screenplays were, as they say in the business, under consideration. I did substitute teaching in New Haven to make ends meet.

This was between husbands. Before my little girl was born. A perfect child. I remember how terrified I had been when I was pregnant. I had seen all those children in classes for the trainable mentally retarded and I was afraid for her.

I can recall climbing up that hill in New Haven and facing a rectangular brick structure. It was a clear spring day. The sky was a deep blue and filled with high billowy clouds that floated by effortlessly. The school had the bland architecture of urban schools with children's drawings taped on the windows in an attempt to cheer the gray, leftover-meat quality of its walls. With narrow, barred windows and a metallic entrance door, it looked like a jail or an insane asylum. Like here.

The children weren't allowed into the building until the bell rang at eight, so children and parents gathered around the school doors. A man was crying outside the gate because his little girl started school that day. I wondered what was so bad about that.

The assistant principal, Mrs. Hurley, a big woman with brown spots on her pale skin, had a bunch of keys clipped to the side of her leather belt. They jangled as she strode down the halls. After the necessary introductions, she escorted me to the classroom.

"You have a group of eight children," she explained while she glanced at her watch. She spoke as if the words were stuffed in her mouth.

"Eight to twelve years old and functioning at a very low level. They're toilet trained and can feed themselves, but that's about it. Can't teach them any more than that. You know, self-help skills. Some are Down's syndrome, others severely brain damaged. Just keep them calm and follow the regular teacher's lesson plan. Our teachers prepare a week's lesson plan just in case they're absent. If you follow it and keep the kids busy, you won't have any trouble. Understand?"

She had the teacher's mannerism of shaking the index finger at the person she addressed, while the rest of her hand made a fist. Teachers start doing this deliberately, but by the time they have taught for ten years or so it becomes a habit of which they are no longer aware. I could bet that Mrs. Hurley did it when talking to herself or on the phone.

"If you have any difficulty, here's the intercom." Mrs. Hurley took a few long steps to the wall. "Dial 3 and I'll pop in to help, if I have the time." She looked around the room, then glanced at me a bit skeptically.

"Better go down now, the bell's about to ring."

I studied the plan. It was neatly written with specific activities for each hour of the day. What the hell was gross motor coordination? I asked myself. And I thought this substitute teaching was going to be an easy way to make some money.

I was pulling teaching materials out of the classroom closets Mrs. Hurley had unlocked, when an aide brought in the children. All eight. They sat in their color-coded desks. Well, they recognized colors, I thought. That must be a hard thing to do. Or maybe it was the concept of color that was difficult to grasp. How would I know? Maybe they were all at the wrong desks.

Among the drooling, swaying children sat a child who looked entirely out of place. His desk had a green dot labeled Francisco. I checked the attendance sheet. Eight children on the rolls, eight children at their desks. No absences. On my only day here, wouldn't you know? When I called all the children's names, only Francisco, who had been scrutinizing me with big dark eyes, responded by raising his hand.

"Francisco," I said. He smiled and said nothing, but his eyes sparkled. "*Ven acá*," Come here, I said in Spanish.

The boy walked up to my desk and I continued to speak to him in Spanish.

"What's your full name?" I asked him.

"Francisco Morales Rosario."

"I'm Miss González. I'm your teacher today because your teacher couldn't come to school. So, where do you live?"

"19 Sullivan Street."

"How old are you?"

"Ten."

"How long have you been in the United States?"

"A few months. We came from Puerto Rico. My father was here for a long time working before we came. And he had to save money to bring us."

"What's your mother's name?"

"Adela Rosario de Morales."

"Do you have any brothers and sisters?"

"Two brothers. I don't have any sisters."

"Do you speak any English?"

"Not yet, but I'm learning some things in school and on television."

This was my self-fashioned intelligence test. Based on my own judgment, this child was nothing but a normal ten year old.

I noticed the noise level in the room increase. Two kids were slapping each other in the face and one was rolling on the floor moaning. The swaying and drooling of the swayers and droolers was getting progressively worse and some of the droolers were making gurgling sounds deep in their throats, laughing and stamping their feet.

I put an arm around Francisco's shoulders and asked him to sit down.

"Okay, children, it's time to do some work. Everybody, sit at your desks, please."

I clapped a few times, since no one but Francisco was paying any attention to me.

Madre mía, I thought, this is going to be a long, long day.

When the aide took the children to the lunchroom, I picked up after them, the room was a mess by then, and went to the desk to search through the children's folders. Each folder had an educational plan and assessments done by psychologists, social workers and special education specialists. I pulled out Francisco's file. Just as I thought. His IQ test had been administered in English, a language the boy couldn't understand. Jesus, in this day and age, don't they know any better? I thought. His IQ was reported in the trainable mentally retarded range. I would be classified mentally retarded too, if someone gave me an IQ test in German. Couldn't the psychologist see the sparkle in the boy's eyes?

Clutching the file, I was halfway to the principal's office when I heard a terrible high-pitched scream coming from a closet.

"Don't mind her." Mrs. Hurley stood next to me at that moment. I had been so distracted with the scream, I didn't hear her keys jangling.

"It's the new girl. Started having tantrums the minute she stepped into the building. Can't understand English, so we can't reach her. Had to lock her up until she learns to behave herself."

"I can calm her down," I said quietly. "Put her in my class and I'll take care of her. At least for today."

"You think so?"

I nodded.

"Well, okay, but you have a handful without this behavior problem."

Mrs. Hurley pulled out one of her keys and unlocked the closet.

A little girl, who was no older than ten, cringed in the darkness. I spoke to her as gently as I could.

"Why are you so sad, *linda?*" I asked in Spanish.

The little girl looked up. Her face was tear-stained.

"Come on, I'll take you to my room, okay? There's a boy there, Francisco. You can talk to him, he's really nice."

She gave me her hand and we walked out of the closet.

"That's great!" Mrs. Hurley cried. "This child has been a real problem from the minute she got here."

"She doesn't speak English and can't understand why she's here. She's just frightened, that's all," I said.

"What does it matter? She's retarded, in English or Spanish or Chinese. That's why she's in this special school." Mrs. Hurley suddenly got defensive.

"Well, I'm just a substitute teacher."

"That's right, you're no expert."

"May I have a look at her file, just to see what her educational objectives are, and then I can maybe work with her a little this afternoon." I smiled my most innocent smile.

"Well, I don't know. Suppose there's no harm to be done by it."

Don't count on it, I thought.

When I looked at her file, I realized that Liliana had been tested by the same psychologist who tested Francisco, in English, of course. Someone was out there making sure all the Puerto Rican kids who filed past his desk were safely put away. This was one of the worst cases of child abuse I had encountered during my time as a substitute teacher.

I gave the other children some busywork to do with clay, and they slapped it delightedly on their tables and unstuck it to slap it down again. They would be entertained with this small chunk of clay for hours. Maybe. If I was lucky.

In the meantime, I sat in a corner with Francisco and Liliana. At first, Liliana had refused to enter the room when she saw the other children, but just as she screwed up her face to start crying again, I got Francisco to bring her in.

The next morning, I took out my credit card, which I kept hidden under my underwear for emergency use only, and took the shuttle to Washington, D.C. That's where I met Jaime, at the Department of Justice. I supposed, correctly, it turns out, that there would be someone in that office who had some notion of what justice was. Secretaries, assistants to this-and-that shunted me around for half the morning, until I finally alit at the Division of Civil Rights. And there he was, sitting behind piles of papers, cradling the telephone receiver with his shoulder while he took notes on a yellow legal pad.

To make this long story a bit shorter, Jaime and another Civil Rights lawyer took a statement from me as complainant, swooped into New Haven to investigate, confronted the school administrators with their evidence and they managed to get Francisco and Liliana retested, in Spanish, and placed in a regular bilingual program. Happy ending.

✳ ✳ ✳

Amazing how I can recall this episode so vividly. So many stories woven into stories, spiraling in time to eternity.

But I still can't remember what happened to Jaime. He would visit me, if he were here. Wouldn't he? Maybe he's in Washington. The distance between us could be a problem. I can't ask Dr. Rhodes either because I pretend that I remember everything. Never know what he'll be up to next. These injections make me feel so strange and alienated from my own body. Some of my recollections are as crisp as an animated movie. Somehow they don't seem real. I'll tell Dr. Rhodes about this incident I remember so vividly. That should earn me a few points.

Points for what? This isn't a game. Or is it?

III

Dr. Rhodes, with his neck sticking out of his collar like a duck, came to my room to inform me of yet another increase in my injections. They keep us informed of these things, as though we had any choices. We don't and they know it. And we know it. The injections are the latest treatment for my problem, he said. In their code that means they're experimental and he's using me as a subject. To test them out. It's easier to destroy than to construct.

I feel very strange. Afraid of things I can't name. Sometimes I can stare at the fold of a curtain for hours and find it the most fascinating thing in the entire universe.

After my shock treatment today, I had a flash. What I call one of my memory flashes. I'll recall something, but as though it were a dream, not as something I have experienced. It's like watching a film in which I'm the protagonist. And I stare at myself and in my initial confusion, I think I have somehow managed to leave my body and examine my entire life as it rolls in front of my eyes like a movie reel. But then, how can I see all of this, if I have abandoned my body and my eyes are now on the stranger I see playing my role in the dark theater? A terrible fear grips me at those times and it takes me hours of trembling and weeping to calm down.

✦ ✦ ✦

This is what I remembered today. Jaime and I traveled to a tiny village in Naples once. It was quiet and quaint. One day I woke up at dawn and, while Jaime still slept, I took a walk through the dewy mist before my first espresso. I turned into a narrow cobblestone alley. The houses had red slate roofs and potted geraniums on the porches. It was a scene straight out of medieval times.

I stood at a corner and had an urge to look up when a middle-aged woman came out to the second-floor balcony of a house, her hair covering her chest all the way down to the waist. Dreamily, looking out into the distance, she brushed her long black hair and then swept it in a knot at the back of her head. That's when I realized she was bare-breasted. Big brown breasts, like country bread loaves, sparkled in the morning sun. I just stood there staring at her, wanting so badly to press my face against her breasts and take in that aroma of freshly baked bread. I almost cried. Then she stepped into the house and the spell was broken. I'll never forget her, despite the injections and the shocks and everything I've been through since then. Yet she doesn't even know that I exist.

This flash pitched me into the deepest of sorrows. I suddenly remembered what it feels like to be happy, to ache for something you want so badly you can taste it in the roof of your mouth, to stare unflinchingly at something beautiful, to want to live another day.

I had forgotten what it was like to hope.

✴ ✴ ✴

I asked Dr. Rhodes today when I can go home.

He said not for a while.

I said, what does that mean?

He wouldn't answer me, which made me very angry.

I told him, in no uncertain terms, that my husband was a lawyer, and he couldn't keep me here against my will.

He said, what husband?

I said, Jaime.

He got up with that fake look of concern he likes to summon up every once in a while. He said, you're hallucinating again.

That's what he says when he catches me in a lie. Which really confused me, because I wasn't lying this time. I just wanted to get out of here. No more lies, no more anything to get around him.

Now, you know that you haven't been feeling well with this new treatment. That's all that's going on. Just go back to your room and rest. We'll talk about this later.

Then he patted my hand.

※ ※ ※

The sound of rain, hard and insistent, pounds in my head relentlessly. I can't sleep on this wet night. My heart is cold and damp, I can feel the outside of myself, a spectator of my own life. A nurse wanted to take the photograph I had in my pocket away from me, and I tore it up and flushed it down the toilet.

I don't know who I am anymore. What is me? The worms are back slithering out of my eyes. I have to keep rubbing my eyes and picking at them so I can write. I have to keep writing, I have to keep writing, keep writing. Writing. My brain is hemorrhaging. There's blood everywhere, but the worms lick it up. They're licking up my brain.

Oh, out there in the black rain, there's a rim of light. No, oh, no, it's fire! I can smell the flesh roasting. I have to get out of here, I have to get out. Out. Out of here.

※ ※ ※

Oh, no, no, no, there he comes, followed by a struggle of people. His white coat flapping, his neck craning out of his collar. A nurse holds up a hypodermic needle. Shush journal, be quiet. They'll all go away soon.

"You Ain't Black You Ain't White You Ain't Shit"

Tried to cheer myself up after work today and bought a lovely bouquet of orange gladioli at the Korean deli. I usually buy irises, they're so serene, but today I felt the need for something more exuberant to get me out of this funk. Turns out it wasn't a wise decision. A gladiolus tip poked me in the eye and my contact lens popped out. So there I was in the middle of West Broadway, on hands and knees, yelling, "Everybody freeze!" Like in an action movie.

It's been one of those weeks. The kind you wish you could erase with a long hard swipe. I'm expecting the kettle to whistle any moment now. Can't wait to have a cup of camomile tea and drop off to sleep. After I rinse my eye with some Collyrium, that is.

My eye's throbbing still. Tomorrow's my day off and I had planned to stay in bed, just to be sure I wouldn't experience anything the least bit eventful. Thought I'd draw the curtains so it would be night all day. That way I could make the beauty of the night last longer. I like that about the night, just staying awake and watching it. Cars flit by like moths under the dim light of street lamps and not one human voice can be heard. The night sparkles with stars I can't see from my apartment window, but it doesn't matter. I can feel the pull of those stars, wandering through the sky. Knowing those stars are there, dotting the world, makes me feel at peace.

As I was saying, the way this week has gone, I didn't want to do anything that might involve the slightest risk like, heaven forbid, reading magazines in bed all day (which I would make into night by keeping the curtains drawn). Something dreadful could happen, like turning a page and suffering the deepest paper cut in history while engrossed in the latest how-to article for curing bongo skins, which is the kind of stuff I read when depressed. This in turn would require an emergency blood transfusion and stitches. Or worse, I might have fallen out of bed and cracked my head on my wooden clogs. As you can see, I wasn't in a very optimistic frame of mind.

As life would have it, a drunken bum on the subway on my way home this evening changed my dark mood and my determined intention of wallowing in it for days. Isn't life funny that way? A chance encounter with a totally pathetic character can have the power of transforming everything, including the funk I was in. Just like that.

The week started out all right. On Tuesday morning the alarm clock went off on time and the weather was good. So it wasn't hard to leave my warm apartment and go to work. Stepping out of my building that morning, I took in the fresh scent of spring. The refreshingly cool air mingled with the misty morning light. That seemed like a promising sign, better than any horoscope could offer. At the corner, Benny was already biting into his belt and using it as a saxophone, playing some off-key riff from the corner of his mouth. So I smiled to myself, glad that some things were just as they always were. But, just as I turned on Bleecker Street with a little bounce in my step, humming a little tune (compliments of Benny the Belt's inspirational performance), the jarring wail of a car alarm intensified to an unbearable pitch. A young man wearing a red anorak dashed by the noisy car, pitching eggs at the windshield. There's a war raging in New York now on account of the racking effects on people's nerves caused by car alarms. New Yorkers are taking the matter into their own hands, smearing wailing cars with rotten eggs or gluing bumper stickers on the windshields with Crazy Glue.

I ducked into a café for a quick cappuccino before work. When I went out again, my nose started twitching, a definite indication that the ragweed count was high. Since even non-drowsy formula antihistamines knock me out, I expected a miserable day at work, allergy-wise. This did not bode well, considering the boss I have and the kind of work I do, catering to the pedicured feet of snotty customers and pretending to enjoy it.

Although I have a degree in filmmaking, I work in the retail business to pay the bills. Like so many other people in the city who are really actors, musicians, artists, but survive on waitressing or driving taxis. I like living in New York. Everyone here is really something else, from somewhere else.

I came to New York to run away. Into my own mind. Before that I lived in Boston for many years. Boston's a cold city. Even in August when the weather is so hot you can fry an egg on the pavement, a chill, deep in my bones, was always there, reminding me of my absolute loneliness. The interminable winters were hard, snow crusting the streets like a biker's helmet, a snow so drab it made my eyes hurt and tear just to look at it. The gales of Boston tunnel between buildings all winter long, sharp as knives, cutting into your face and vulnerabilities. I used to gaze at the gray Charles River, take long walks down Fresh Pond, bicycle through the Cambridge Common, but I was blind to the beauty other people saw in the city. I always felt outside of myself there, having strange doubts about my identity. It was in Boston that I was forced to define who I was and couldn't find the vocabulary. It was there that I began to doubt myself, to see myself in the angry eyes of strangers who refused to see, to know, to acknowledge the person that I was. My mind wasn't free to really reach into itself and roam its interior landscape. I was always distracted fighting something or other out there where I didn't want to be in the first place. In Boston I felt like a graft that doesn't take.

I call Boston the city of snow and slurs. Racial, of course. The slurs, not the snow. I was always picking slurs off my skin there. A place where I could never belong. My mother and I wound up there when she got a scholarship to go to graduate school. And she had to take me along, what else could she do? At times I wished she had left me with my grandmother. While there, I kept looking at snapshots taken back in Puerto Rico where I had been happy, just to remember what happiness was really like. It was one of the things that kept me going.

Not belonging anywhere is a problem, except in this city. New York harbors everything and everyone. It is tolerant, nonjudgmental and forgiving as a mother. I reconciled with my own self here. To me New York signifies a return to the self, where identities are enhanced, strengthened. New York is populated by people who wander endlessly in their own minds. And I feel at home here. By New York I mean Manhattan, of course. The Village specifically. I only venture uptown to work.

Attending film school in New York was a good option for me. I hate to write, except scripts, because in a screenplay you can say it as it is. That's why I'm talking instead of writing. I'm better at it. I like to read though. Stuff like contemporary Lebanese women novelists (in translation, of course) and African women's poetry. Anyhow, I had no interest whatsoever in an academic career. I'm too visual. Besides, I've hated school since kindergarten. I remember when I learned to read in the first grade and got so distracted with the process, I couldn't concentrate on the reading itself. I kept asking the teacher, why does c-a-t mean a cat, why isn't it d-e-p or x-m-g? The teacher phoned my mother to complain about my lack of discipline. I never did well in school because of this distractibility, as teachers called it. I was always thinking about other things or wanting to draw purple clouds or cut up a picture book to make a paper village. It was off-task behavior, the teachers informed my mother accusingly. Whatever that means.

Film school was different. I could go off on tangents. In fact, I was encouraged to do so. My student films were all about tangents, becoming distracted on the way somewhere with interesting happenings and experiences, so that arriving never became the target. My films never had a point, in the conventional sense. The point, of course, was everything that was going on. And my professors actually understood me! So, I really got into it.

I didn't have to read to memorize facts, either. Instead, books started to fill my mind with images and lots of metaphors. One of the most exciting moments for me was discovering hidden meanings in the way words were put together. Then I realized I could become a translator, from ideas to words to images. Cool.

I also learned a lot about film as an art form. I remember the first foreign film I saw was *Iphigenia*. I'll never forget the scene where the Trojan men wait for the wind to come up, naked on the white sand, sun pounding on their muscular backs. In this scene, Achilles, who was handsome as any Greek god, lies on his stomach. Slowly he raises his head and chest like a regal serpent and ever so gently blows on the white sand. The sand he lifts with his breath fans out in a spume of gold dust. The beauty of that scene was so overwhelming, I walked around for days with the image in my mind.

Film school was really neat and at the same time I could escape from Boston without being too far from my mother. *Mami* lives alone now, pretty much settled in Boston with her job and a house in the South End. Somewhere along the way, she stopped being my mother and became my friend. It's weird. We'll talk on the phone and she'll say things like, don't stay out too late when you go out at night, as though it meant something. It really does and it doesn't. She knows I'll come home as early or as late as I want. Maybe she just needs to remind me of who she is, as if I could ever forget. Sometimes it's so hard to realize how separate we've become, and I wish we could come together again in that halo of oneness we once lived in when I was a little girl. Now, she wakes up in the morning with thoughts I can never penetrate, having had dreams I'm no longer a part of. And I live my separate life too, making daily decisions, hoping that what I do is right. Sometimes I have to hold myself back from phoning all the time, asking her, is this okay? Do you approve of my choices? I really care about what she thinks of me. Once I bought a CD of some particularly misogynistic rap music. I really didn't care about the lyrics, but the beat. I had barely left the shop when a disturbing thought hit me. What if I was run over by a car and my mother got my remains? She'd be so disappointed in me. So I rushed back to the shop and returned it.

I wonder at what moment our separateness became real and we drifted away from each other's wombs like strangers swimming in the vastness of the sea. I used to know where she was every moment of the day. And she was in touch with me at all times. Now, we connect through telephone wires and don't see each other for long stretches of time. Somehow I feel deep inside that we've both lost something irretrievable.

Well, despite our independence, I still worry about her. She accuses me of reversing our roles and treating her like my daughter. I'll scold her when she tells me about the long hours she spends at the lab and when she complains about something physical, but won't go to see a doctor. She ignores me completely, of course. Now I know how it feels. I've been doing the same to her all my life.

Mami's had lots of boyfriends, but I haven't liked one. She says I'm just jealous of any man who comes near her, but I think her choices have been pretty dismal. When she falls in love, she's blind to her lover's many flaws. Luckily, I've always had my eyes wide open and been more than willing to point out all the shortcomings she misses. Thank goodness, considering her appalling taste in men, she's never been serious about anyone, not even my father, who disappeared early in my life and whom I never got to know. I have a feeling she used him to have me. Then she went her merry way. In the end, *Mami* says she'd rather live with her insects. What can you expect from an entomologist?

I don't know that much about men and I have a hard time sensing how to act when they're around. I always feel constrained somehow. There weren't many men around when I was growing up, so I never got used to things like putting the toilet seat down. My mother was an only child brought up by her widowed mother in Puerto Rico. I was brought up by them in a small cement house in Santurce, on Avenida B, to be exact, with a balcony boxed in by the same style of iron grills that protected all the jalousie windows. I didn't even have granduncles. Ours was a world of women. They used to call us Amazons in our neighborhood. I'm not sure they meant it to flatter us.

To top it off, our next door neighbors had five daughters. The mother, who must have loved to travel in her imagination, named them after the continents. So my friends were

Asia, Africa, Europa, América and Australia. Luckily, they left the name Antártica for last and, after Australia, didn't have any more daughters. Can you beat that for living among Amazons?

I don't remember lots of details about my very early childhood, I think my father was still around then. I recall that when I was about three years old we had a cat that lived in the garden and he used to catch mice. Every time it caught a mouse, my mother petted it and said, "Good kitty." I got so jealous of the cat, who was taking my mother's affection from me. So one day I found a mouse the cat had killed and discarded under a bush in our garden. I took it in my mouth and ran to my mother. I thought she'd be so happy and proud of me! To my great disappointment, when she saw me and what I was carrying, she started screaming at the top of her lungs and almost had a heart attack.

The only man who seems to linger in my memories of childhood is Celestino. He did some gardening and odd jobs around the house. He made me laugh so hard when he hung lizards from his earlobes like earrings. The continents nextdoor used to shriek and run into their house when he did this. But I loved it.

Celestino had a habit of sticking a pinky into his nose and turning it around like he was searching for some hidden treasure in there. This habit got him into a lot of trouble once. He got carried away at a New Year's celebration and fired his *compadre's* gun to the sky. A neighbor called the police and they summoned Celestino to court for breach of the peace. My mother went with him to give him some moral support because he was so nervous and he didn't know anything about legal things. Not that she did either, but he said that she was *leída,* well read, because she had been to university. He was real nervous when he was told to stand by his court-appointed lawyer and, as he usually did when he wasn't thinking, he dug a finger into his nose. The judge got real angry, slammed his gavel, and ordered Celestino to cease and desist from putting his finger in his nose or he would sentence him to thirty days in jail for disrespect in a court of law.

Despite his habit, which I imitated for a while until my mother took me to task for it—in Puerto Rico it's called taking bread out of the oven—I had a good relationship with Celestino. We were both religious rebels. He listened attentively to my stories about the repressive regime of the Irish-American nuns in my school and nodded knowingly. While he weeded the garden or repaired a faulty hinge, he contributed his own enthusiastic anecdotes about the antics of drunken priests. Celestino's priests were always Spaniards and always drunk, but my nuns were always American and always severe. I guess this reflected the generational gap between us.

Anyhow, I got along better with Celestino than I do with the men I've run into recently. Actually, my love life is a real joke. Two years ago I was engaged to Julien, a French guy I met in Aix-en-Provence on one of those student-exchange trips. He was a film student too. We had a great time together, but he had a terrible temper. Once we drove to Normandy and stopped at a restaurant for lunch. I know the French are trendy and love gimmicks, but this was too much. We went in and faced yellow-gray walls full of paintings of battles, complete with bombs exploding, soldiers throwing hand grenades, the whole bit. At the tables, they had placed Walkmans so customers could listen to military marches while eating. The menu was on a view master and included items like Hiroshima Tartar, Atomic Filet, Bananas Flambé à la Pearl Harbor. I can't remember what we ordered, but it tasted like a petroleum derivative, really plasticky. Julien was convinced the food was frozen. He took one taste and bolted out of his chair.

"This food is *merde*," he yelled at the waiter. "I'm reporting you to the police." He was waving his arms all over the place. "You tried to poison me with this food. This is attempted murder!" His arms wheeled like a windmill and his eyes were wild and white.

Before the waiter could argue with him, Julien grabbed my wrist and dragged me out.

Well, Julien and I fell madly in love (does one ever fall in love any other way?), and three weeks later he proposed. When I returned to New York to settle everything before returning to France for the wedding, I wrote him long letters, in French because his English was even more abysmal than my French (don't ask me how we managed to communicate). He used to say things like "wrist clock" instead of wristwatch. Anyhow, I'd write about my longing for him and all those silly clichés people in love use as though no one had ever said them before. He used to return my love letters having circled in red ink all of my grammatical mistakes. You know how the French are about their language. Okay, so I did write everything in the present tense, but that's how I spoke French. No big deal, I just never got around to the other tenses. Anyhow, by the time they were returned, my trans atlantic letters looked like they had caught the measles. You can imagine what happened next. Our engagement didn't survive his grammatical vigilance. I wouldn't take it from the nuns and I certainly wasn't going to tolerate it from a fiancée, no matter how cute he was. I haven't quite recuperated from that experience yet. I'm really not sure what I expect from men. Unconditional love, maybe? I hope someday I can figure it all out.

❖ ❖ ❖

As I said, my mother's an entomologist. I remember how horrified she was when my friend Asia used to play with me in our garden. When Asia got restless, she'd poke in the ground for ants and pop them into her mouth, soil and all. In my nightmares she would swallow the ants whole, and they would land in her stomach still alive and crawl around and then slither out through her nose and mouth. When I told her about it, Asia said, no way, that she liked to bite into ants because they were so crunchy, and they tasted much better when she chewed on them. I was really relieved to hear that the ants were crushed to death by the time they reached her insides. Unfortunately, my mother was listening and gave us a lively lecture on the importance of ants in the scheme of things. I think Asia felt really guilty and never ate ants from our garden again.

On account of ants, my mother loves Luis Buñuel. Before he became a filmmaker, Buñuel wanted to be an entomologist. That's why ants and other insects appear so much in his work. I can tell when *Mami* watches the parts in *Un Chien Andalou* when ants crawl all over the palm of a guy's hand. That's when she pushes up her glasses and bends closer to the TV set. She has a Buñuel video collection and she can identify all the ants in his films. I always know when she's seen a Buñuel film because she'll start telling me about the 10,000 different species of ants known to scientists and how ants have been around at least 100 million years. She thinks they're fascinating. Ants are her specialty, you see.

I have a feeling she likes ants because she admires the self-sufficiency of the queen, who lets herself be fertilized during a nuptial flight. Right afterwards, the male dies, so the queen sheds her wings and founds a new colony. I think my mother identifies with this female autonomy. By studying ants, she says she can understand herself better and also the needs of humanity to nest, prey, gather, enslave others and even march in huge columns of armies, devouring everything in their path. It's no wonder she's such a pessimist. She can get weird on me sometimes, let me tell you.

❖ ❖ ❖

Well, getting back to my week (see what I mean about going into tangents all the time?), as soon as I got to work last Tuesday, everything started going wrong. Early in the day my boss, the shoe designer Nola Berlin, you may have heard of her, who has got to be the most neurotic person I've ever had the misfortune of encountering, decided that I was like some kind of curse to her. Even before she heard me sneezing and sniffling on account of my allergy.

She bounded into the boutique and went straight to the cash register where, nose dripping like a faucet, I was counting the meager sales we had made that day, hoping I'd sell a lot more shoes by closing time. Counting sales is what you do in a store when you're bored.

"What's your sign, Teresa?" Nola demanded to know with a wild look in her eyes. She had gum wadded up inside her cheek, like a plug of tobacco.

"Scorpio," I answered, really puzzled by this time.

"I knew it! Don't even talk to me today. Antigone said the solar eclipse hit my sign and Scorpio is gonna drain me till I'm dry. Get out of my way!"

"But, Nola," I said, running after her and sniffling, "we have to discuss the summer displays."

"Never mind that," she waved frantically. "I can't see you or talk to you today. Tomorrow. Maybe. Just stay away from me, all right? And take care of that cold, will you? You look dreadful."

"Sure thing," I said, stifling a sneeze.

What else could I say? Nola had almost fired me last week because of a disagreement over astrology. She stormed into the boutique just as I had finished talking to a customer on the telephone.

"What is the meaning of this, Teresa?" she yelled.

"Excuse me."

"This, this." She waved a trade paper in my face. "I told you to put in an ad for a sales clerk and I specifically told you that the ad should say that Libras need not apply. Libras and I are totally incompatible. Then, the first thing I do this morning is interview a girl and, of course, she's a Libra. I hate Libras," she hissed. "They're so goddamned balanced!"

"But, Nola," I said, "you'll have a lot of trouble if you print an ad saying you're excluding a group of people. It's discriminatory."

This only infuriated her more. She was almost spitting when she managed to respond.

"Wait just one minute, young lady. Whose side are you on anyway?" She slapped the paper on the counter and put her fists on her hips. "What are you, a bleeding-heart liberal? What the hell do I care about any of that? This is my business," she pounded her chest with her fist, "and I can hire anyone I please. Here I am struggling to protect myself, and you're sabotaging me left and right. I should fire you right this minute, you know that?"

Too bad she didn't fire me. Then I would've qualified for the kitten I wanted.

On Monday, I had decided to stop by the ASPCA to pick up a kitten. I had always wanted a pet, but because of what happened to me with Rocky the parakeet when I was a teenager, I was reluctant to make the commitment. I'm twenty-five years old now and my experience with poor Rocky has faded a little. Having put Rocky behind me, I called the

ASPCA and asked if they had any homeless kittens, and they said sure, that I could pick one up anytime.

The animal shelter is way uptown and it took me forever to get there. The brick building was next to a huge housing project and it sagged all over the place like the jowls of a very old bulldog. Inside, powder blue paint chipped from grimy, mildewed walls. The decor was definitely low budget. Lots of plastic, Formica and gray color schemes that didn't match at all with powder blue. The reception area had a strong odor of caged animals. I took a peek inside the room where the cats were kept segregated from the dogs. Some of the older cats were lying still in their cages. Others came up to the cage bars and stared at me full of mistrust. I felt oppressively lonely. At that moment, I wanted a kitten so badly, my womb ached.

A slight, bald man approached the counter. He had the raspy voice of a smoker and asked me very politely whether he could help me. He took me into his office and gave me a form to fill out. His white shirt had long vertical and horizontal creases as though he had taken it right out of a new package. He was very nice until he read through my application. He shook his head gravely with a disapproving look.

"I see here that you work. How many hours are you away from home?"

"All day," I said honestly, not knowing this was a trick question.

"Well, I'm sorry," he huffed. "You're not eligible to take one of our kitties. There's just no way someone who works full time can take care of a young pet."

"Excuse me," I said, raising my voice a little too much, "but is there anyone in all of New York City who has the luxury of being home twenty-four hours a day to take care of a kitten?"

"As I said," he enunciated slowly as if I was deaf, "those are our rules. Kittens can get into trouble, like bite an electric cord, or scald themselves on the radiator. Lots of things can happen."

"What do you do with the kittens you don't find homes for?"

"Well, um, we put them to sleep."

"Oh, all right, then, that certainly makes a lot of sense," I said, hoping my sarcasm would have some effect. It didn't.

I was so shocked at being declared an unfit kitten owner, so unfit that the ASPCA would rather gas a kitten than give it to me, that I almost suspected the true reason was that they had somehow found out about the hapless Rocky.

I was a junior at Cambridge Alternative High School when Amita, my best friend, asked me to take care of her parakeet Rocky while she went away for a weekend with her family. Amita and I were really close. I envied her a little because Amita had a father, a mother, two sisters and a little brother. That seemed ideal to me. Her mother always wore beautiful silk saris, even in the winter, and oiled and perfumed her hair with some kind of jasmine oil that smelled wonderful. She invited me to dinner all the time. The meals started off with puffy naan, straight from the oven. Then Amita's mother would bring out platters of chicken tikka or lamb curry, split green lentils and lots of boiled rice. During those meals, I would pretend I was part of the family too. To this day, the sweet smell of curry reminds me of Amita and her family.

Amita was the first friend I made when my mother and I moved from Puerto Rico to Boston. I was only ten years old then. Amita and I met at Cambridge Alternative Elementary School. My mother was always putting me into alternative things. It's a hangup she has from the 60s. Well, I really can't blame her. Guess she thought it was the best way to deal with my school phobia. I really truly hated school, especially when I was forced to learn English. I struggled so hard not to get lost in the harshness of the language. I also feared deprivations I was sure I would suffer when I learned it. I became even more terrified of English when my grandmother, who came to visit us from Puerto Rico as we were settling in, heard me practicing some words I had learned in the new language. She hugged me and said sadly, "When you learn English, Teresa, I'll never be able to speak to you again."

I really got upset because I loved my grandmother so much. When I went to my mother crying and expressed to her my fears, she explained that just because I learned English didn't mean I had to forget Spanish. I could have both. I was really relieved.

But when I started speaking English well, I realized that often I'd forget the names of common things in Spanish. No matter how hard I tried to remember, the Spanish words just wouldn't be there perfectly arranged in my mind the way they used to be. I was so distressed about this that one day I went to school and refused to speak at all. I didn't speak for weeks, months. My mother was practically pulling her hair out, but it wasn't so bad. Since I wasn't distracted by words, everything seemed sharp and vivid. All my senses seemed to have awakened from a deep sleep. That's when I began roaming in my own mind, searching for hidden rooms, furniture covered with white sheets, and the dusty attics of memory. I've never stopped.

My mother, who has a practical nature when confronted with any problem, big or small, took me to a child psychologist. Dr. Thomas represented another authority figure I could add to my list of oppressors (you know, with the nuns, the English language, teachers in general). At this point, *Mami* wondered whether she had failed me in her motherly duties by allowing me to develop the language of rebellion, which is what my silence was. But how could she control it? Despite my mother's efforts and that stupid Dr. Thomas, I curled into myself like a mimosa when it rains and hid all the words I knew deep in the folds of my mind. I clenched them so tightly they couldn't escape. I hoarded the words like a miser, shook my head in anger and hurt, stamped my feet until the psychologist was out of my life.

When the sessions with Dr. Thomas failed miserably, *Mami* decided to put me in the alternative school. Then my grandmother came from Puerto Rico to live with us. I came out of my silent cocoon one evening when my grandmother was tucking me in and asked me, ever so gently, "Do you love me, *mi niña?*" Without realizing it, I whispered, "*Sí, abuelita,*" and fell asleep. The next morning, I sat down to have breakfast, opened my mouth and almost fell out of my chair when I heard my own croaking voice. I could hardly recognize it. My grandmother pretended this wasn't a big deal and chatted on about this and that as if nothing had happened. *Mami* had already gone to work, so she got the news less dramatically over the phone. I never forgot Spanish again. Even after my grandmother died some years later and, during her funeral, I felt that I was eating stones and raining so many tears I would flood the entire world. Her space will always be in me, unfillable. But it's not a void. It's hard to explain. Every so often I get the strong urge to run to her and ask her advice about a guy I've just met or whether a certain outfit suits me. She's no longer with us, but she is.

I missed her so much. Especially when I dreamed in English for the first time. It was so sad because I realized that I had made an irreversible jump into this strange, foreign language. My native language hurt me after that. Sometimes I'd wake up in terror, yelling words in Spanish, words that remained quiet and still on my tongue during the long days of foreign existence. It was as though my grandmother and my mother tongue were one. I seemed to miss the same tenderness from them both.

I still miss her.

Amita and I were friends from elementary school all through high school. Now that I live in New York and she's in graduate school in London, we don't talk very often, but we still write. We're both dark-skinned, but in the color scheme of Boston we weren't considered black, and we weren't considered white either. We were in a sort of racial limbo. Once my mother was livid because at school they categorized us by race, so my ESL teacher put me in the Hispanic-Black category and my homeroom teacher in the Hispanic-White. My mother stomped into the principal's office, clutching the offensive student information form and asking, "What is the meaning of this?" When the principal realized why she was upset, he asked her, sarcastically I thought, what race we belonged to. "The human race!" my mother cried. The principal shot a glance at the door, hoping someone would rescue him from this peculiar woman. I had been ready to crawl under the carpet.

Amita and I weren't accepted by our black peers and even less by whites. Luckily, we found each other. We understood right away that we had fallen into some kind of crack where we had lost who we were and where we had come from. Amita never talked to me about India and I never talked to her about Puerto Rico. We were trying so hard to be just like regular kids. But in the beginning, we really didn't know what regular kids were supposed to be like. Then we discovered them in magazines and television programs. That's when we understood that regular was not a word meant to describe us.

Amita and I shared lots of secrets when we were growing up. Like the time we went to Mass and took Communion, though neither one of us had ever attended catechism or made a confession. Amita, of course, had only heard rumors about Catholicism because she was Hindu. I knew little more than she did. My mother was an agnostic and didn't want me brainwashed into any religious belief until I was mature enough to make up my mind. I haven't yet. Made up my mind, that is. When I attended Catholic school that first year of my educational career, she made sure I wasn't required to attend religion classes or go to Mass. I did pick up some of the practices of Catholicism though, like making the sign of the cross—it was inevitable. When *Mami* realized that despite her best intentions, Catholicism was worming its way into my consciousness, as she put it, she pulled me out of the nun's school and put me in a Montessori program, I think. More likely it was Piagetian. I'm sure my mother would have trusted the educational ideas of Piaget, the zoologist, better than Dr. Montessori, who was just a medical doctor.

Anyhow, there were lots of Catholics in Boston, and Amita and I were curious about what went on in their churches. So we went to Mass one Sunday morning, dying to taste the host, and for some reason we thought we'd get to drink wine too. You can imagine our disappointment when we realized that the priest chugged down all the wine and we were left with a wafer stuck to our palates. We had a hard time unsticking and swallowing it too. And it was really tasteless. A definite "not worth it."

Amita was also responsible for trying to introduce me to the mysteries of sex. She was a year older than I and, at thirteen, had already had her period. She even showed me her sanitary napkin once. I thought the whole thing was gross. Once, we lied about our ages and snuck into the local movie house to see *Saturday Night Fever*. After explaining what it was that the protagonists did in the backseat of cars, Amita reassured me that it was all right to "do it" as long as you were standing up. Then a girl wouldn't get pregnant. Making out in the backseat of a car would definitely lead to some terrible consequences, according to Amita. At the time, I had no idea how to "do it" anyhow, but I filed the information away for future reference.

But getting back to Rocky, you know, the parakeet. Well, when Amita's family was about to go to Cape Cod for a few days and Amita asked if I could sit with Rocky, I agreed. Dutifully, I wrote down instructions on his proper feeding schedule, changing the newspaper at the bottom of the cage, covering the cage up at night so Rocky could roost undisturbed by light. It seemed like an easy task at the time, but has anything ever come easily? I ask. Of course not!

On Saturday all was well. I clucked at Rocky a few times to keep him company while he paced in his cage and flapped his wings. I let him sort of nibble at my finger playfully. His tail would flare when I scratched the back of his neck. He was really weird-looking, though. His lower beak protruded over the top part, so he looked like a thug or a boxer. Something like Sylvester Stallone in that boxing movie. That's why Amita called him Rocky. Anyhow, Rocky spent an uneventful day on his perch on Sunday and at times he'd roam up and down the bars of his cage, beak, claw, beak, claw. But he wouldn't eat or drink. I didn't think anything of it. As far as I knew, parakeets ate every other day, sort of like pythons eat a rat or a bunny once a month.

In the evening, he started acting real strange. He thrashed against the bars of the cage, squawking and fluffing his feathers. His feathers were flying all over the place. I slipped the cover over his cage, hoping darkness would lull him to sleep, but he kept pounding and thrashing and squawking until my mother reminded me it was bedtime. (She knew a lot about ants, but about as much as I did about parakeet behavior.)

You can imagine my distress when I rushed to the cage the next morning and removed the cover. There was Rocky lying on his back, frozen like a tiny porcelain knickknack, feathers slicked back, tiny legs sticking up like match sticks.

"*Mami,*" I yelled. "Something's happened to Rocky!"

My mother peered into the cage and poked the by now stiff bird with the tip of a pencil. "He's dead," she said evenly. (You know how direct and matter-of-fact mothers can be, especially when you can use a little beating around the bush.)

Well, I cried my eyes out. Here was my charge, entrusted to me by my best friend in the whole world, and now he was dead. I was definitely not to be trusted. As the ASPCA undoubtedly found out.

When Amita came to pick up her parakeet, I had to break the terrible news.

"Oh, no, " she cried when she heard my story. "Rocky was used to flying around our apartment all day. He only went into the cage to sleep."

"Why didn't you tell me that?" I asked, trying to control myself. I was ready to burst out crying too. "I would have let him fly around."

"I thought your mother might mind," Amita swiped clumsily at the tears streaming down her face.

"Amita, I think he committed suicide," I said after thinking it over for a while. "He preferred to die than to live in a cage." (I had a tragic sense of existence, even then. I think I get it from my mother.)

My mother's only comment, with that wry sense of humor she's worked hard to develop, was that I should someday write a book entitled "Gruesome Crimes of the Century" and include a story about a girl who drives her parakeet to suicide. Hey, Ma, don't rush so much to jump on the bandwagon of animal causes!

Well, that certainly did nothing to cheer me up. Neither did the fact that the number-one hit those days, which you had to be dead to escape from hearing, was Rocky's theme song, "Gonna Fly Now." Every time I heard it, I cried my eyes out.

So, Rocky committed suicide, and I wasn't deemed fit to adopt a homeless kitten. Although these events may seem unrelated to you, I have a strong feeling that one thing definitely has something to do with the other. I don't know what, though. Is it my basic pessimism at work? That cumbersome trait I get from my mother?

My mother, as I said before, has a bleak outlook on life. Reading the newspaper every morning only confirms her worst expectations. Her favorite philosopher was burned at the stake by Italian Inquisitors and her favorite contemporary author has a *fatwa* on his head. A few months ago, she gave me a book by this very same author, warning me to disguise the cover if I was going to read it in public.

Well, just this week, wouldn't you know, I got around to reading it. Ignoring her advice about disguising the novel, I took it to work so I'd have something to read on the subway. When I got out at my station, a man rushed up to me, raincoat flapping, and wagged his finger in my face.

"What're you doing reading that junk?" he demanded. "Don't you know that man's a blasphemer? All he writes are packs of lies."

"But it's a fairy tale." I explained lamely. "Fairy tales are supposed to be lies."

The man gave me a withering look. "Shame on you." he said and stomped away.

I love fairy tales. That's why I studied filmmaking, to invent my own. I'm also a self-taught percussionist. I like to invent my own rhythms. When I was small I reacted to the *boleros* my mother listened to all the time by banging on any hard surface I could find, including my head, with her chopsticks. My mother got tired of my beating rhythms on her polished mahogany table (maybe she worried about my head too) and finally drove to El Barrio in New York City to buy me some *timbales*. On the way back, we stopped at the drugstore and she got herself a pair of earplugs. Over the years, she made lots of trips to El Barrio to get me congas and bongos. She said it was important to go to real Puerto Rican musicians to purchase them.

Eventually, I taught myself to play everything from maracas to the marimba. While other kids were listening to the Bee Gees, I was saving up for Mongo Santamaría albums. My mother kept playing her *boleros,* but I wouldn't hear them any longer. I only heard the beat of drums in my head, even when I slept. Don't get me wrong, I have nothing against *boleros*. It's just that Carmen Delia Depiní, Virginia López, Blanca Rosa Gil, and all the other sad-voiced women my mother liked to listen to made me feel real down. In those terribly sorrowful songs, they pleaded to their men to take them back after they had dumped them for someone else, to lie to them and say they loved them even if they didn't. In fact, these lyrics were open invitations for abuse. It's no wonder Latinas are so messed up when it comes to romantic attachments. We're brought up expecting betrayal, deceit, infidelity from men, and hope, like beggars, that they'll throw us some crumbs whenever they feel like it. No thank you! I tell you, I beat on those drums so hard, I almost drove my mother and myself crazy. Better crazy than a hopeless martyr, I thought.

I'm trying to raise money to make a film about a society in which violence doesn't exist because everyone's a musician. In their parks and plazas they have statues of composers and musicians instead of generals and soldiers. Whenever there's a conflict, people solve it musically. For example, if there's a war, soldiers receive orders to "Bring up your oboes, on the double!" And they march to a spot overlooking a peaceful lake and play their reeds until exhausted. Or during a particularly nasty argument, a husband might say to his wife, "I'll smack you with a G-flat so hard your aria will wilt." I'm working on the script now, but you get the idea.

In the meantime, I have to put up with Nola, who's always pushing us to sell, sell, sell. On one of those many occasions when she deemed we weren't selling enough at the boutique, my colleague Brenda and I were just standing around chatting while we waited for someone to come in, when Nola tore down from the workshop practically foaming at the mouth.

"What're you two babbling about? Get to work!" she yelled. "Why isn't there anybody in here anyway?"

Brenda pointed her chin at the lashing rain outside. "It's been slow today, Nola. The weather's lousy."

This infuriated Nola even more. She waved hysterically toward the street while she yelled at us. "I don't care what you have to say. It's not the weather, it's not the economy, you gotta sell. What are you doing wrong? Ask yourselves that. Look at all the people out there! Tons of people are dying to buy my shoes. You just gotta get 'em in here. Go on, go out there and get 'em!"

Brenda and I glanced out just as a little old lady, wrapped in a shiny yellow raincoat, limped by the boutique window with a small mutt on a leash. She was the only soul on 56th. When I looked at Brenda, she was staring out the window, her face set hard, but her shoulders shaking from laughter. Nola didn't appreciate her hilarity and fired her. "*Ciao, bambina,*" was how she put it.

※ ※ ※

The day Brenda was fired, my friend Sofía had called me at work to invite me for a tequila. I really didn't feel like going. I was so depressed about what happened to Brenda. But Sofía was happy because she had gotten a new job managing a *botánica*, a new upscale spiritualist store, and she wanted to celebrate. After work we met at Temple Bar on Lafayette Street. Her eyes sparkled in the dim room. We ordered tequilas and some nachos.

"Boy, do I feel pooped. You wouldn't believe how busy I am, Teresa," she said excitedly. "Managing a *botánica* is like nothing I've ever done before. Especially keeping it supplied with the merchandise we need." She became more and more enthusiastic while I was going into a fast fade.

"Get a load of the things I have to keep in stock: graveyard dirt, coriander oil, sulphur and ammonia crystals. All that stuff for magic spells is great!"

Suddenly, I perked up. "Hey, Sofía, what do you recommend to get a neurotic boss off your back?" The evening might turn out to be quite auspicious after all, I thought hopefully.

Sofía considered the question. "You can try the Boss Fix Powder we carry."

"What's that?"

"Okay, now let's see." Sofía put up her hands and counted on her fingers. (You could tell she was new at this.) "It's a combination of musk, chili powder, tobacco and pulverized newsprint. We blend it all in the right proportions, you know."

"No kidding. And what do I do with this concoction, slip it into her coffee or something?"

"You really don't know anything about these things, do you, Teresa?" She looked at me skeptically.

"Hey, I'm a fast learner."

"All right," Sofía said patiently. "All you do is sprinkle the powder around your boss's office and around your own work area for seven days. And *voilá,* your boss leaves you alone."

"I don't know," I said doubtfully, "it sounds too complicated. How about a plain old-fashioned knife in the back?"

"Too messy. I'll bring you some of the powder. Doesn't hurt to try."

"What if Nola catches me? Then, it's *ciao bambina* to me."

"Let me know if you decide to take the plunge into the unknown," Sofía said.

"Do you really believe in that stuff?"

Sofía shrugged. "Who the hell knows what to believe? But hey, if a person really believes that something is going to help her, it will. It's not the power of herbs and powders, it's all in the mind."

I nodded dully. I could feel the tequila had gone to my head.

Sofía glanced at her watch. "Listen, Teresa, I better go and get ready for this date I have."

"Who's the lucky guy?"

"Ugh, he's a rep." Sofía sounded disgusted. "You know, for magic supplies. Well, he has the hots for me, and I have no interest in him. But I have to string him along because he carries the best chicken feet in the country."

"Listen," I said laughing, "maybe you'll have a good time."

Sofía rolled her eyes up to the ceiling and sighed. "Yeah, right. We'll talk about the comparative merits of black devil candles versus wormwood powder to get rid of an enemy. Fascinating. It's all right at work, but on a date..."

"Hey, next time make sure you fill me in on this black devil candle stuff. Sounds easier than the powder. You know, to fix Nola," I said hopefully.

Well, it's already Saturday and Sofía hasn't gotten around to getting me the black devil candles or even the Boss Fix Powder. Whenever I call her, all I get is her machine. It turns out she's been going out with the magic supplies rep every night this week. She finally called me from work yesterday to let me know she wasn't dead or anything.

Why is it that we women always do that? The minute we get involved with a guy, we dump our women home from work this evening, I had been thinking about Sofía and her rep and poor unemployed Brenda, who was a little spacey but a nice person, and my neurotic boss. After she fired Brenda, I got busy rearranging the boutique, for something to do, when Nola returned with some sketches under her arm.

Showing me a sketch, she said, "I'm working on a new design for the Fall. What do you think?" She sounded really insecure when she let me take a look at the rough sketch, that frankly, was nothing to write home about.

"Should it be hot pink, bright red, and should it be suede or patent leather? What about the heels? Mid-heel, high-heel, platform, wedge? And the toe, pointed or square? Well, what do you think?" But she continued mumbling before I had a chance to respond.

"I don't know," she said with frustration. How can you know what they'll go for? Jesus, women are so fickle."

"I think orange is going to be the "in" color next season, and rounded toes, definitely!" I said before she started mumbling again.

Nola stared at me for a long time. I felt she could drill a hole through me and a chill went up my spine. She turned her back on me and looked around the boutique area I had just finished rearranging. She waved her hands dramatically, sweeping them across the room, like a Wagnerian diva.

"And what do you think this is? Does this look good to you?" She looked at me angrily. "Well, it doesn't look good to me." And she proceeded to rearrange the area, right in front of the customers. Then she stomped out.

Well, that's the last time I give you my opinion about anything, I thought.

I was so weary at that stage, that I could have just sat right there on the floor and cried, hugging all those fancy shoes to my chest. But I had to drag myself to a customer who was waiting. I brought the shoes she wanted in the size she requested. When she tried the shoes on, she walked around a bit, but looked undecided. Trying hard to persuade her to buy the shoes, I said, "You know, these shoes look really good on you and they're so comfortable, aren't they? You could walk miles in them."

My sales pitch wasn't working. The customer looked dubious. Wouldn't you know, at that moment Nola appeared out of nowhere, with a scowl on her face. She lashed out at me right in front of the customer.

"What are you saying?" she asked me and snatched the shoe box from my hands.

She turned to the customer. "You gotta excuse her, she's new here and doesn't have a feel for my designs. These shoes aren'sale. Just to teach me a lesson, I bet. She was practically on her knees begging the customer to buy. But it didn't work. The customer gingerly removed the shoes and slipped on her own. She shook her head at us both and bolted out the door.

"Now look what you've done," Nola yelled and pointed an index finger at me, almost shoving it in my face.

"I can't believe this! Are you stupid or what? Don't you know anything about effective sales techniques, after all I've taught you? Jesus! I can't believe the things you people say when you're selling. Crap, it's all a pile of crap." And she rushed off mumbling under her breath.

✦ ✦ ✦

What a day. I was so tired on my way home. So very tired. My knees stung a bit from scraping them on the sidewalk while searching for my contact lens, which I never found, by the way. My vision wasn't too acute because I only had one lens on and it was already dark out. The gladioli bunch gave me reason to pause, so I carried it as far removed from my face as possible. Despite everything, I was relieved that Nola hadn't fired me yet, I needed the money, and though I didn't have a kitten, I considered the possibility of buying a goldfish or some other living thing that wasn't under the iron-fisted rule of the ASPCA. A parakeet, though, was out of the question, for obvious reasons.

I was grateful to find an empty seat on the subway. My feet were killing me and I slumped in the seat with a huge sigh of relief. I cautiously placed the flowers on my lap. A young man, with jeans and sneakers, was standing by the door, listening to his Walkman. Then he started getting into the music. At first he bobbed his head up and down, slowly, then faster and faster. Then he started moving his torso and the rest of his body. He was dancing salsa, I could recognize the moves, but only he could hear the music. Suddenly he really gets into the music. He gets down, and starts turning and dipping and making all the fancy salsa moves. He went on in a frenzy, oblivious to everything around him. The other passengers looked up at him with indifference. This is New York, after all, and everyone has to carry a "no big deal" expression at all times.

I was sorry to see the dancer get off. I started glancing through a filmmaker's magazine I had picked up on the way to the station. I got involved in an article on nonlinear editing—that's just a fancy way of saying editing with a computer—when the slurred voice of a man intruded into my consciousness and I couldn't concentrate, no matter how hard I tried to push the garbled voice down as deeply as I could into my subawareness. Reluctantly, I looked up.

Sitting across from me was a middle-aged man wearing crumpled clothing and staring at me brazenly. He reeked of cheap wine, piss and vomit. Through his torn trousers I could see that he wore nothing underneath. I had read somewhere that the homeless don't wear underwear because no one thinks to donate intimate items of clothing to charity.

The instant I looked up, he took in my brown skin, curly hair and the other characteristics that reveal the different races that course through my blood. He shook his head dolefully from side to side.

"Look at you," he said to me accusingly and poked a filthy finger in the air as if he were pecking on wood. "I don't get it," he shook his head. "Look at you, look at you, look at you." He paused to recapture his elusive focus. "All these black women marrying white men and having weird-looking kids like you. Like that Diana Ross bitch having white babies. Man, you all bitches."

Great, that's all I need, I thought. I glanced down at my magazine again, flipping a few pages, though the words I stared at so intently ran into each other in a blur of black streaks. I regretted not bringing my Walkman. With some of Tito Puente's salsa, I would have drowned out the drunk's voice. I might have even joined the subway dancer, if I hadn't been so tired. That's what I should have done. It's hard to be depressed when you're dancing salsa.

I kept my eyes firmly set on the magazine, but my preference for reading over the drunk's tirade only made him yell louder about the indignities of black women mating with white men. Why he assumed my mother was black and my father white, and not the other way around, is a mystery that could only be explained by his own past, I suppose.

He stopped to catch his breath, then pulled out a half-empty bottle of wine from his jacket pocket and took a slug.

"Ugh, stuff's horrible." He screwed up his face. Then he took another swig and smacked his lips. "Ha, ha, ha," he pointed at me again. "I'm black, but you, bitch, know what you are?" He laughed and reeled to the side, almost falling against the passenger sitting next to him.

At this point, and to my immense relief, the train pulled into my station.

"Look at you," he yelled, as I rushed out of the train, clasping the wilting gladioli tightly to my chest, thanking my lucky stars I'd be home soon.

"You ain't black, you ain't white, you ain't shit!"

※ ※ ※

It feels good to get back to the sanctuary of my apartment. To the musky smell of overwatered ficus and ferns, the dirty pots left to soak overnight in the sink, my script-in-progress waiting for me on the kitchen table. The drunk's words still ring in my ears like cymbals. I look at myself in the full-length mirror behind the bedroom door and separate my skin colors, like party ribbons: one black, one brown, one white.

It's true that I'm not black and I'm not white. But those aren't the only colors in the world. And it's certainly true (though the drunk didn't mean it that way) that I'm not shit either.

Hey, I'm not doing so badly when you think about it. I make a living. True, it's not doing what I want and I do have to put up with Nola Berlin, but maybe I can get a grant somewhere to do my film. In fact, tomorrow I'm determined to work on the script. The salsa dancer would be a great character. So would the subway bum, if I could make him drunk on Respighi, for example. Then he'd harass people on the subway with bars from *Feste Romane*. I've been accused of torturing people with Respighi myself on many occasions. I wonder if I could introduce a glockenspiel in there somewhere...